Into Wild Sherwood

by

Edie Roones and M.A. Lee

Tod the Fox and the Faeries in the Ring
The Poisoner and the Faerie Huntsman
Three Yule Feasts for the Faeries
Friar Tuck and the Faerie at the Pool
Alan-a-Dale and the Harp of Elandrielle

WRITERS INK BOOKS

Tod the Fox and the Faeries in the Ring

The Poisoner and the Faerie Huntsman

Three Yule Feasts for the Faeries

Friar Tuck and the Faerie at the Pool

Alan-A-Dale and the Harp of Elandrielle

All Copyright © 2022 Writers Ink Books

First publishing rights: April 2022

All rights are reserved.

DISCLAIMER

This book is a work of fiction. The names, characters, places, and incidents are products of the writer's imagination or have been used fictitiously and are not to be construed as real. Any resemblance to persons, living or dead, actual events, locale or organizations is entirely coincidental. The author does not have any control over and does not assume any responsibility for third-party websites or their content.

First Published in the United States of America

Cover Illustration by Deranged Doctor Design

www.writersinkbooks.com

winkbooks@aol.com

Into Wild Sherwood ~ Dangerous Faeries Lurk in the Forest

Pursued by the Sheriff of Nottingham and his guards, five people take refuge in the wilds of Sherwood Forest ~ only to encounter the Faeries of British legend.

~ ~ ~

"Tod the Fox and the Faeries in the Ring"

Never enter a Faerie Ring. The Faeries like to play.

With the guards of Nottingham on his heels, Tod flees to wild Sherwood Forest. Frightened in the night, he falls into a Faerie Ring.

Faeries play with their catch, whether in the Ring or on the Wild Hunt. How can he escape them?

~ ~ ~

"The Poisoner and the Faerie Huntsman"

Never reveal weakness to a Faerie.

Escaping a false accusation of poisoning, Melly and her hound seek refuge in Sherwood Forest ~ yet the Nottingham guard who accused her is on her trail.

That night, she encounters the black hounds of the Wild Hunt. Then the Hunstman arrives. Has she fallen into greater trouble?

~ ~ ~

"Three Yule Feasts for Faeries"

Will the cook become the final dish?

Yule, the worst time of year for Ellen Best. Few buy her breads at Market. No one will hire her for their Winter Feast.

Then a Faerie knocks at her door. Two dinners, he proposes, and a final feast for his duchess. After each, she'll receive three purses, copper and silver and gold.

What did the Faerie mean by *final* feast?

~ ~ ~

"Friar Tuck and the Faerie at the Pool"

No one escapes a Faerie.

After visiting the hermit of Sherwood, Friar Tuck seeks the coolness of a forest pool. There he encounters a Faerie.

She is wondrous and strange and deadly. How can he convince her that he is a man of peace, unlike the guards and rangers who hunt in the forest?

~ ~ ~

"Alan-a-Dale and the Harp of Elandrielle"

Who can trust a Faerie?

The song competition at Nottingham's Winter Feast offers a purse that will pay Alan-a-Dale's debts. He wins the first night's round ... offending his competitors who take revenge.

At his lowest point, a Faerie finds him. She offers him a bargain— yet who can trust a Faerie?

Contents

Tod the Fox & the Faeries in the Ring

"Got ya!" The guard crowed his triumph, but Tod twisted in his grasp. He aimed a fist where it would hurt. The boy's punch wasn't hard, but the big man flinched. Tod jerked away, and his tunic tore. He staggered but quickly caught his feet and darted into Nottingham's market day crowd.

"Hi ya! Stop that imp!"

Tod dodged away from a farmer, slithered between two foresters, and bounced off a hand cart, spilling early-season apples to the mud. The apple seller shook his fist.

He saw two guards ahead, talking to a brown-robed clerk in scarlet stockings. They heard the shout and spotted his guilty dash. The men shifted position to block the street.

Tod gambled and dove under a passing wagon. The mud softened his fall but slicked under his feet as he scrambled out the other side. He came up between two market booths and bear-walked to reach the building behind them. There he crouched, panting like a dog.

Where to run? Where to go? His ma and sisters were gone, smuggled away in a cart three days after his pa's arrest for stealing, when they all realized no one would help his pa. The sheriff's captain had confiscated their wagon and the cob, along with all their possessions, from the Golden Arrow inn. They were homeless. Pa faced charges for stealing, and the guards had harassed Tod's sisters for the fifth time.

Tod had remained in Nottingham while his ma and sisters escaped. He had vowed to help his pa, no matter what his punishment. Pa hadn't robbed anyone. They earned that coin with their minstrel act.

He had hung around the keep's entrance, hoping to catch a glimpse of his pa or discover when the annual assize would occur. The guards hadn't liked him hanging around the keep's gate and ran him off—until they guessed that he knew where his ma and sisters had gone, bound for another town where his ma had people.

His family had come for the big market day. They intended to make coins with his sisters' songs, his pa's fire-breathing, his ma's juggling. Tod did tumbling. They'd made the coins, a pouch full, and planned to leave with the dawn. Then the captain came with his accusation of theft. The guards arrested Pa. And the harassment began with the next dawn.

For a week he had run free on the streets. He encountered urchins, slippery eels with no more protection than Tod himself had. The host at the Golden Arrow had already risked himself, finding a way to get Ma and Else and Frenny out of Nottingham. He knew no one else.

Tumbling had saved him ever since they began chasing him this morning. The guards wanted to catch him, and the only reason he could figure was to discover the location of the coins they had earned or to discover where his pretty sisters were hidden.

Pressed against the wall of the building, Tod shoved a knuckle in his mouth to smother a sob. He was a big boy, Pa said, no longer a little boy who cried. He earned good coin with his tumbling. He'd helped Ma and Else and Frenny escape. He'd promised he would lie low until Pa came to the assize court. That thrice-bedamned captain had no reason to charge Pa. Every coin in that pouch they'd earned. God's Grace that Ma kept the bulk of their earnings, and the coins they'd taken off Pa were just takings since noon.

The double-stacked barrels obscured his view of the street. They also hid him, giving a few minutes of safety. As soon as the cooper moved one of the barrels, though, Tod would be exposed.

He shoved his knuckle deeper as another sob threatened.

The salty smell of frying pork tempted his stomach to growling. Market talk was the same here as anywhere. He used to like hearing the noise, the hawking, the bargaining, the gossip. He didn't like it now. He listened for the guards. He surely hadn't escaped them so easily.

Maybe he should creep away, using the space between the booths and the building to escape.

Then he heard "Where's the boy? Did you see the boy? Scrawny bag of bones. Red hair. Little thief. Where did he go? Which way? You sure?"

The questions drifted away.

Tod wanted to peek over the barrels, but his red hair was a banner. His stocking cap, knitted by ma, was in their wagon, lost to him now. He began to squirm from behind the barrels. He bumped one, and the one on top teetered. He held his breath. It settled. Breathing again, he crawled out of his hiding place.

Where to go? He began to crawl behind the booths to reach a different lane.

Then one of the shielding barrels was lifted away. "Here now. What's this? It's that boy!"

Tod didn't wait to see if the guards were close. He pushed up and ran into the crowd. And into a guard's back.

As he rebounded, the guard whipped around, prepared to cuff him. Then the man saw his banner-red hair. "Here! Here he is!."

Tod ran, back the way he'd come. He passed the apple seller trying to wipe mud off his apples. He slipped between two couples and slithered past a stout merchant.

He got tangled trying to get around a passel of youths. They had a May game of pushing and tugging him, swinging him round before passing him off to a mate. He'd get one arm free only to have it snagged when they spun him another way.

One youth missed his catch. Tod sprawled across a booth.

Fingers tangled in his hair, holding him in place. "Get on with you" came a woman's hard voice. "Pestering folk. The guards are coming. You won't like how they pester you."

The youths catcalled and shouted insults, but they retreated.

Tod tried to stand straight, but those entangled fingers weren't letting him go.

"In here," the woman said.

"Lemme go."

"In here," the woman insisted. "The guards are coming. Crawl over."

She gave him a tug and then a haul, and he was up and over the booth.

"Under this," and she pushed him down.

He found himself under the booth bench, crouched against the outer wall with a dark drape offering cover from her side.

"Stay there," she hissed.

Then he didn't know what she did, just that she bustled away to rummage in something.

The pork smell filled his nostrils. His mouth watered. His stomach complained of emptiness at the lovely smell of fresh bread.

"Where is he?" The guards still followed him. "Which way did he run? That red-headed boy?"

The questions neared, and Tod held his breath. Then they moved on. He breathed again and waited in the close darkness. For the first time in days he felt safe. He could see the woman's clogs, wood farm clogs, the toes tipped with mud.

The drape lifted. She handed him something. Then she straightened and twitched the drape into place.

It was bread. Two slices. With a slab of ham between them. He bit into the offering. It was half-gone before his head caught up to his stomach. He slowed down and savored it.

With his head working again, he heard the conversation above him. Guards, and him separated from them by two thin boards.

He lost his appetite. It pummeled him when he heard the voice. "Caught `im earlier."

"They said you helped the boy." That was a different man.

"Wastrels, the lot of them, apprentices off their masters' leash and up to no good." The woman's complaint sounded like all the old crones who'd ever harangued Tod. " `Course, I helped the boy away from them. Not half their size. You need to talk to these apprentices. They're always tumbling someone."

"You making a complaint?"

"Not this time. Don't want to make it official."

"Where did the boy go?"

"I didn't see. I wanted him gone. Those `prentices left him laying out over my booth. He knocked my loaves. Here, you look hungry. Sausage roll? Just a bit to buy two."

"They said you had a hand on the boy."

"Only long enough to keep him from knocking everything to the mud. I have pasties. That's a bit for one."

Coins jangled.

"Where did he go when you released him?"

"Like I said, I didn't see. I had to fix what he messed up. I've a honey cake here. One bit."

"How did you miss that red hair?"

"I've got my living to make, good sir. The last tax bit me hard. Melly?" she called. "You see where that red-headed scrap went?"

"Cross the way, wasn't it, Huon? Aye, cross the way. He was keeping away from those `prentices. They're a right menace to good folk. Tell your captain, good sir."

A voice from the booth's other side agreed and asked for the captain to come. The man wanted to make an official complaint. "Why, just last market day—."

"I'll be on my way," the guard said.

Tod's stomach settled. He nibbled at the bread. He heard the Melly woman hawking her seeds and dried herbs. The woman kept standing before the drape, blocking his escape. Two customers bought pasties and a sweet bun while he finished the ham and bread. Belly bulging, he smothered a belch. He wanted to curl up and sleep—but the market wasn't safe.

He tapped the toe of her wood clog.

She shifted her foot. She started talking to a couple interested in a whole honey cake.

Tod waited until the couple left then rapped her shoe again.

She knelt. "Be still. He's watching." She pulled out a basket beside him, taking away some of the yeasty smell, then she straightened.

Tod played finger-twiddles to pass the time, but it was no fun without his sisters.

The drape lifted. She tossed something at him. "This will hide that foxy head of yours." Then she was back to her business.

The something was a stiff felt cap, shaped and sewn to fit snugly on his head. It smelled of lavender and rosemary. He tugged it on and fingered around the brim. The cap hid most of his curly red hair.

The women were helping him, not just hiding him. Tears pricked his eyes.

"I'll go now," the other woman said.

"You're a wonder, Melly."

"Say that when I've found him. Golden Arrow, you said?"

"Likeliest place."

Were they going to fetch the host? The man had already done enough. And he wouldn't be happy to discover that Tod hadn't left with his ma and sisters. But he couldn't abandon Pa, and there wasn't room for him in that cart. Removing his thin body had ensured Ma and Frenny and Else stayed hidden.

The next time the drape twitched aside, the woman tossed in a tunic, better than his, too big. He cinched the neckties tight so it didn't hang off his shoulder. In smoothing it into place, he discovered a thicker band around the bottom edge. Shifting around to put the edge into a shaft of light that came through a tear in the drape, he saw an embroidered edging in a color slightly different from the tunic. He made out a hound, several hounds running. He couldn't see more than that.

The woman drew back the drape. She had crouched, and he had his first good look at her, the silver-white hair, her rounded face, and rosy cheeks. "Your tunic," she demanded.

"You're helping me. Why?"

"Fair play."

"You can't go the host at the Golden Arrow." He bundled up his torn tunic and thrust it at her.

"We're not."

"He's already——."

"You're lucky you were there, not at some of the other places. Be still and quiet a bit more, boy." She straightened before he could say anything. In seconds she was back down, shoving an empty basket beside him. "What's your name?"

"Tod."

She grinned. "Tod the Fox. That name I'll remember."

"What's yours?"

"Ellen Best, but people call me Best Cook." Then she popped up with a speed that belied her white hair.

His next wait was short.

Melly had returned. "Watch for it. Rander brought his big saw."

"And?"

"He's waiting at the postern. He's sent word into the forest."

The forest. Tod shivered. Wild Sherwood Forest. Outlaws

and wolfsheads hid there. Faeries caught people who were never again seen.

He and his sisters were frightened and cowered inside their wagon when Pa and Ma drove them through the wild forest that surrounded Nottingham. The coins they might earn over a month of markets had forced this venture. And look where that need for coin had gotten them.

Were these two women planning to send him into the wild wood?

"May I borrow a basket, Best Cook?" Melly swept aside the drape.

Tod offered a basket.

The young woman dimpled. "You're a sweet one," she whispered. "Do you know the cow bar gate? And how to get there without walking in the middle of the street?"

Not for nothing had he had days running with the Nottingham cast-offs. He nodded.

"That's where you need to go. Look for a man in a brown friar's robe. He'll get you through the gate without attracting attention. Then he'll direct you from there. God speed to you, Tod." She took the basket and straightened.

Tod drew the drape into place.

Maybe they weren't sending him alone into wild Sherwood.

He was back to playing finger-twiddles when Best Cook twitched the drape and hissed for him to come out. He straightened, wincing from leg cramps, and bent to massage them.

Best Cook pushed a bundle at him. "Here. I'd wish you Godspeed, but it's not God who'll be looking after—Hello, good sir."

Her eyes had widened. Tod didn't dare turn.

"After more honeycake? Go on with you." She handed Tod a bulging sack and shoved his shoulder. "Back to the friar. Tell him I thank him for his business. And don't dawdle."

"The apprentices said you grabbed the boy."

"Grabbed a boy? I certainly did not."

Tod ducked through the booth's side opening. Arms crossed over their girth, two guards stood before the booth, once again questioning Best Cook.

She gave smiles; they returned frowns. "You grabbed him," the scowly one said, "and hauled him into your booth. Like you knew him."

They ignored Tod. As he walked past, Best Cook offered a lie. "I know no red-haired brats. I wouldn't want him back here with my food. He'd eat all my profits."

Melly motioned frantically for him, and he veered into her booth. She gave him a half-shove to the back of her booth. "This way."

He ducked through a hanging cloth and saw a narrow opening between the buildings. He glanced back. Best Cook was trying to press more honeycake on the guards.

A breeze came through, fluttering the weaver's cloth. The movement caught a guard's attention. He spied Tod watching and elbowed his mate. "That him?"

The other guard cursed then shouted for his fellows.

Tod ran.

The byway twisted. He emerged from the alley to a crossing, a lane with more people going about their day. His alley continued on the other side. He skipped across the lane and plunged back into the narrow alley.

He trundled along at a good speed, wary because every crossing risked a lane or a street where the guards might be. The town walls loomed over the buildings, keeping his direction sure. When the byways finally tossed him out beside the wall, Tod hesitated to leave the close alley. Peering out, he saw that he had managed to reach the postern gate. That wasn't the gate he needed. He retreated to the alleys again and worked his way around a quarter of the town.

He thought himself lucky to avoid the guards.

When his byway ended, he had reached the wide gate that admitted wagons and drays. The cow bar was open, swung to one side, and two guards leaned on the gate and talked while people passed to and fro.

Near the gate, pawing through the contents of a pony cart, was a man in a brown gown stretched tight over his round belly. A fleece of blond curls grew wild and tangled while that bald spot on his head gleamed. The cart looked as old as the friar, rickety, its short planks warped and badly hammered in place.

Tugging at his cap, Tod trotted to the weathered cart and fetched up at the friar's elbow. "I'm here, sir. Best Cook sent this." He handed over the bulging sack.

The friar jerked then grabbed at his chest. "God's wounds, boy, don't sneak up like that. Here, hold this." He seized a bucket from the cart and shoved it at Tod. A worn leather pouch nestled in the bucket, its strap curled on the top. "Put your cap on it, boy," the friar hissed.

"My name's Tod."

"No. I don't want to know." He walked to the harnessed mule and stroked its nose. Tod didn't think much of the harness job. The cart had a singletree, and the friar had yoked it loose, nearly dragging the ground. Nor did the mule have a girth that would help it pull. "Now, we want to get to the forest, Ruby. Let's start now, easy and smooth."

The mule tossed its head and began pulling. Tod jerked off his cap and threw it atop the pouch.

The cart swayed from side to side. Its wooden wheels rumbled over the cobbles. The guards turned to watch their progress. They covered their mouths to speak, likely criticizing the harness but not wanting the friar to hear. Neither man moved until the friar and his mule reached the gate.

"Here, you, where you going?"

"To the forest. The abbot at Thurgarten Priory wants mushrooms."

One guard levered himself off the gate to peer into the cart. Tod hung back, not wanting to attract attention. "That's a crowded cart for a mushroom hunt."

"The abbot also requires that I visit the Sherwood hermit. These supplies are for his benefit."

"Eh, Oswin, we might need to tally those supplies for the sheriff."

"No, no, no," the friar said. "The abbot will provide any tally for the secular ruler of the town, but the Church requires that her ministers are unencumbered by mortal representatives."

"Berne, what'd he say?" Oswin asked.

"May I pass? I have God's work before me, and I'm behind on my prayers for Sext and Nones."

"Sure, sure, go right on. Never say that we interfered with God's minister. The boy will have to stay."

Tod came to an abrupt stop. He took a better grip on the bucket's rope handle and considered the best way to swing it as a weapon.

"What? The boy's with me. He assists me."

"What's his name?"

"Boy."

"Now Tuck," Berne said in a reasonable voice, "that's not the name of the boy."

Oswin started away from the gate, coming toward Tod.

And Tod couldn't move. His head busily matched details. Tuck. A friar. Friar Tuck. Tod stared at the brown-robed friar with his belly advancing before him. There was gossip about Friar Tuck and the Merry Men and Robin Hood. The guards had no doubt heard the whispers. Surely they wouldn't dare act against a man of the church based on suspicion alone.

"We've got a look-out for a boy," Berne was saying. "Red-headed brat."

From Tod's angle he could see Friar Tuck worrying at the

mule's harness.

Oswin came close. Tod moved to the far side of the cart. He pretended to go forward toward Friar Tuck. He kept a tight grip on the bucket.

Oswin followed him.

Then everything happened at once. The mule began kicking and bucking, its hoofs colliding with the loosened harness tree. The friar and Berne ducked out of the way. Tod swung the bucket at Oswin. He didn't connect, but the leather pouch fell out. He flung the bucket away.

"The beer! The beer! Save the bottles!" Friar Tuck yelled.

Berne lunged for the roped-together bottles that were rolling at the back of the cart. Oswin snatched at Tod. He missed his grab, for Tod flipped forward, away from him. He landed in a tangle against the friar. Tuck shoved him away so hard he fell to his knees.

Tuck steadied him and hissed. "The forest, boy. Take the first path to the left. A three-trunked tree. You'll be found." Then he shoved him forward just as the mule kicked apart the singletree.

Tod scooped up the pouch.

The cart had dropped onto its broken shaft. The harness had tangled around the mule's legs. Berne had saved the beer bottles, but a crate of poultry had fallen from the cart and broken. Hens squawked and fluttered and tried to escape. Oswin caught two by the legs and held them upside down while Friar Tuck tried to calm the mule.

Tod ran for the forest and plunged into its dimness.

Within its protective shadows, he glanced back. Oswin still stood with two hens while the other hens ran around his feet. Passersby had joined the melee as they tried to catch hens. The mule had stopped kicking. It stood still while Friar Tuck untangled the reins.

Only Berne, hands on hips, looked at the forest. He gave a low whistle then turned to Oswin, who threw away his hens and ran inside the walls.

Tod took the first path to the left.

After he ran until he was out of breath, after he walked a long way to get his breath back, after the trees began to grow thick trunks and obscure the sky, he began to wonder if he had the right path. He didn't know much about woods. He knew fields and meadows, but he was most comfortable in towns and villages. The trail he followed had looked like a beaten path across a meadow. It twisted back and forth around the trees that grew larger and larger the deeper he ran into the forest.

Twilight gradually fell.

The green canopy obscured the sky. He wouldn't be able to see the moon and the stars.

He still hadn't found the three-trunked tree. Had he missed the trail? He walked and walked while dusk deepened.

He needed to find a safe place. Nothing around him looked safe. What animals would he encounter in the forest at night? He hurried, looking around for the tree, looking for a place to shelter. He didn't even see any trees with low branches that he could climb up. He didn't want to sleep in a tree. What if he fell out?

The wind picked up. It ripped through the green canopy. It flung down leaves and twigs. Broken stubs of limbs dropped with crashes, over and over, before him and behind, off to the side where underbrush had turned dark and scary.

The darkness began to hide the path. He ran on—then the path opened to a clearing, and Tod jerked to a stop to look around.

The clearing was a circle, compact and complete. Thickly-trunked trees created the circle. He recognized oak and beech, rowan and cedar, chestnut and ash and hazel, holly tree and silver birch, all of various heights, all ancient, all just beginning their leaf-turn to autumn. Before each tree was a good-sized rock, big enough to sit on.

Centering the clearing was a boulder, the top flat. Above, the circle cut through the canopy. No branches grew across the opening. The first star twinkled at him.

Faerie Ring.

Tod took a cautious step backwards.

He knew better than to cross a Ring. His ma had warned him to stay away from anything to do with the Faeries.

The trail continued on the other side of the clearing. He would have to skirt the Ring, walking between the circle of rocks and the trees. Two other trails led in. Which way did he need to go next?

A yawn stretched his mouth wide. The day had caught up to him.

He crept to the base of the third tree on his right, the hazel. The ground beneath was dry and mossy soft. He found several nuts on the ground. Cracking them open, he discovered they were ripe. He piled them on top of the rock to add to his food. Digging into his pouch, he discovered pasties and honeycake and a plain bread.

As darkness fell around him, he ate a pasty and half of the honeycake, yawning between bites. He found a stone and cracked a few of the hazelnuts on top of the rock. Then he returned the remainder to the pouch, pasties and cake wrapped in a cloth and the loaf of bread loose. He poured in the nuts and his stone. He slung the leather strap crosswise over his chest then leaned back against the trunk.

When he woke, he didn't remember where he was. Then the wind gusted overhead. A lone bird chirped and chirped. Deep dark had fallen, but moonlight filled the Faerie Ring.

Snuffling came behind him. That must have woken him.

It grunted.

Another snuffle neared. A grunt sounded to his right, a third on the left, then a fourth, all close.

Tod rolled into a crouch. A pair of eyes gleamed. A little lower, he saw another pair, a third, that was a fourth—and a fifth. Pigs. Or boars. A sow with her babies.

Something nudged his back.

Tod sprang away … over the rock and into the Faerie Ring.

Moonlight glowed around him. He turned and saw small bulky shapes, the tusks gleaming in the dark.

Then he was yanked.

He felt poured through a sieve and tried to scream, but dirt filled his mouth. Then he was standing in a great space. He was blind. No one was there—then the space filled. Something crowded against him. People. Many people. Faeries.

Hands gripped his arms and shoulders. They fingered his face, his hair, his hands.

"Look, look," came a musical voice. "Banner red hair."

He yanked in a breath. The air burned cold and dry, scented with greening herbs.

Another one laughed. "He's young, so very young."

Their voices were wrong somehow, human but not, a single tone but not. Tod had heard choirs on feast days. Each one had that multiple voice sound, but he didn't think the Faeries were talking in chorus.

"A mere boy," a man said, the voice above him. His hair was tugged again. "Fox bright. Good for hunting."

He shuddered with fear, remembering stories about the Wild Hunt.

Faeries. He couldn't attack them. He knew no defenses. His ma's warning came to him, bright and loud as the voices around him: "They play with us, like a cat with a mouse. They don't like us."

The pouch was tugged. He kept a hand on the strap. They turned him about, around and around, until he staggered and threw out a hand to steady himself. His fingers touched cold metal and leather and cloth. He still couldn't see.

They laughed and passed him from one set of hands to another and another.

Then everything stilled. He stood alone. No, not alone, just untouched. The Faeries still gathered close. One set of hands turned him, and he saw a twinkle of stars. How was that possible? He was in Underhill, the dreaded Faer land.

"A fine catch, your grace."

Someone touched his hair, a gentle touch, not tugging, fingers threading through his locks. "So wide-eyed," a woman said. "So young."

"So innocent," another said, the voice layered with relish.

"Your name?" said the Faerie before him.

"Tod."

"Foxy Tod." The fingers disappeared.

He belatedly remembered to bow. Flattery seemed wise. "Your grace."

"How do you come to us, Foxy Tod?"

"Something—several somethings came after me in the forest. Boars, I think. A sow and her piglets, I think. Your grace, I did not intend to step into your Ring. My deepest apologies." He heard a step and turned to it, then another and he turned that way. Then a third, and he tried to control the fear that demanded he turn and defend. He bowed again. "Your grace."

When he straightened, a figure all twinkling moonlight and glistening silver stood before him. A woman. *The duchess?* Her shimmering gown was moon-colored. She had styled her silver hair with curling locks over her shoulders, and sparkling pendants and flowers and leaves tucked into her hair. Her skin glowed pale, but her eyes were a depthless dark. Her cheekbones angled sharply beside her straight nose. Her lips looked sooty above her pert chin.

She was strange and beautiful. Those words burst from Tod.

The Faerie duchess laughed. Then she touched his face. He tried not to flinch as she trailed her fingers over his brow and cheeks, across his eyes, down his nose. A light touch to his lips, then she cupped his jaw—and her hand was icy cold.

"We would have great play with you—."

Excited murmurs scared him.

"But we shall not keep you, Foxy Tod." Her hand fell away. "Fenric?"

Tod gasped as his skin returned to warmth. It felt edged and scalded—but how was it hot when her hand had been like thick ice in a frozen pond?

A man came beside him. He looked like the Faerie lady, but he wore armor that gleamed silver in the moonlight—only no moon shone in Underhill. The man grasped Tod's arm. The touch sent cold through his tunic and skin, all the way to his bones, and it stole his breath again. "Come," Fenric said.

Although Tod didn't know how or where, he went.

When he woke again, he lay on a sunny patch of grass. He sat up. He was not at the Faerie Ring but in a different clearing. The sky looked deep blue. Sunshine slanted between the trees.

His arm ached. His jaw ached.

The pouch lay beside him. He drew it close. It no longer contained Best Cook's food. The nuts and his stone were still there. Now he also had a temptingly sweet-smelling loaf. In a shimmering cloth were four dainty round cakes with violets pressed into the top. His mouth watered. A rolled bread stuffed with a tangle of greens had the aromatic scent of the Underhill.

He broke the loaf into four. He ate one piece, then the flower cakes called. The cake was sweeter than honey, light but not crumbly. He relished the first slice. He didn't want a second. He rewrapped the remaining three in the cloth. He considered the bread roll, but he was no longer hungry.

In stuffing everything into the pouch, he discovered a flask. He unstoppered it and took a cautious sip. Water, clean and fresh and sweet. He drank deeply then replaced the stopper and pushed the flask into the pouch.

Then he stood and looked around.

Dew had fallen. The droplets sparkled in the slanting

sunshine. Around him trees grew thick and tall, so he knew he was deep in the forest. A beaten path ran across this clearing.

He took the closer path, reckoning he'd go a ways then come back and try the other.

Birdsong filled his ears. He watched them flit around. Squirrels chattered. A chipmunk sat on a great root then disappeared to safety as he neared. An owl swooped along the trail, returning late to its nest.

Tod ducked. Wings brushed his hair. When he straightened, he saw the three-trunked tree.

He hurried to it. The beaten path widened, creating a gathering place beside the tree. And in that wide space were the ashes of an old campfire.

And just beyond it was another sunny clearing, larger than the one where he'd awakened. The clearing was a circle, with rocks marking the surrounding trees.

He'd returned to the Faerie Ring.

As beautiful as the Faerie duchess was, the others were dangerous. Underhill was a strange place, not meant for mortals.

He backed up and bumped into someone.

A hand clamped onto his shoulder. "Got ya!"

Tod twisted to look up. It was the guard he'd escaped yesterday.

The guard shook him by the shoulder, like a terrier worrying a rat. Tod punched his groin, but this time the guard expected it and dodged.

Leaves rustled, like the wind whipping through, then came a thump. A man's voice snapped, "What are you doing with that boy? Stop shaking him."

Hunched in the guard's hold, Tod jerked around. Beside the oak stood a tall, slender man in green tunic and hose. His hair was ginger rather than banner red like Tod's. A scowl marred his refined features.

"He's a thief. I been chasing him since yesterday."

"What did he steal?"

"Bread. From the market."

"I did not! You just don't like me. You and your mates. I didn't steal nothing!" He swung both fists, but the man had his arm straight, keeping his grip and keeping Tod away from him.

"Shut it, you. You really don't want me mad at you."

"You're a guard for the Sheriff? Only rangers are the justice in the forest. According to King John." The man grinned when he said the last. He stood arms akimbo and head slightly tilted back, looking down his nose at the guard. He had two belt knives and two boot knives. "Best you go back to Nottingham and bring a ranger to arrest the boy."

Is he a ranger?

"Like hell I'll do that. I got the little imp, and I'll keep him. Ranger can tap him once I get inside the walls."

"Rangers won't do that, not unless they see evidence."

"They do what the Sheriff tells him."

The man had no argument for that.

Another rustle and a thump. The guard swung about, taking Tod with him. A second man stood beneath an oak. Dressed the same as the first man, he had dark hair, dark eyes. He was shorter but no less slim. He grinned and drew a wicked long knife, flipped it, then caught it by the handle. Sunshine glinted on the blade.

The guard cursed. Tod took advantage of his distraction to kick. His boots were soft, but years of tumbling had built his leg muscles. He kicked hard, the bottom of his foot striking the man's shin. The guard jerked free.

And Tod somersaulted, gaining distance from the guard. His foot glanced off the man's reaching hand. He flipped forward again—and landed beside a rock. Fear struck him hard. He didn't want another trip to Underhill.

But he got an idea.

He leaped onto a rock then teetered, as if his balance was off. The guard leaped for him, long legs speeding his advance. He lunged for Tod—and missed as Todd jumped to another rock.

The lunge took him into the Ring, almost to the table rock.

Tod sprang from the rock, feet first at the guard who had whirled around to catch him. His feet hit the man's midsection and forced him deeper into the Ring. Tod scrambled back to a rock. "Nyah, nyah! Faerie Ring!"

The man spied the circle of rocks, the circle of trees. Face twisting, he stumbled toward Tod.

Then he disappeared, feet first into the ground. He screamed, but it was muffled when the ground closed over his head. It ebbed away.

The grass wasn't disturbed. The guard was gone.

"Holy Mother of God," one of the men said.

Then a hand slapped Tod's shoulder. "Good work."

Tod turned. The ginger man had reached him. The dark man still stared at the empty Faerie Ring.

"Tuck sent us."

"Are you with Robin Hood?" Awe enriched his treble voice.

"That's us."

"Are you—," he searched for the right word then settled on "safe?"

Jack finally stopped looking where the grass had closed over the guard. "You're safe with us, boy, or we can get you to another town. We don't prey on little boys."

"I'm not little!"

Both men laughed. "Well. We don't prey on those running from the Sheriff and his guards? How's that? I'm Will Scarlet. He's Jack O'Greenleaf. Who are you?"

He sighed, tired of giving his name. He unslung his pouch

and held it out. "I'm Tod. This is Faerie food. Want to share?"

"Not quite here," Will Scarlet said. "Come meet Robin."

And Tod followed them deeper into Wild Sherwood.

The Poisoner & the Faerie Huntsman

In the shadowy room, the vial glowed as Melly stoppered it. Lights sparkled. The magic blinked out as she slotted the vial into her healer's scrip.

She had used more of the magical elixir than she's anticipated. She feared Jonice's husband had noticed the sparkling lights. The elixir emitted no light when applied, only when she corked it.

A rough grunt came from behind her. Melly turned to face the man. In this cramped room with only the fire for light and warmth, the big guard loomed over his wife, who lay on the sole pallet, against the wall. The lamp gave an amber glow to his smashed features. He rubbed his hand over his unshaved jaw.

"She no longer in pain?"

"No pain," Melly agreed. She despised Oswin. She'd tended his wife more than once. The woman stayed only because he followed when she left. *Escaped* was the word Melly would have used. This time Jonice had only broken fingers and bruises. She dreaded the occasions when Oswin truly lost his temper. Her scant magic could speed healing and stop the worst of the pain.

Yet if a body didn't want to heal, she could do nothing. Jonice had not yet reached that point.

Melly would infuse more elixir tonight. Best to be prepared; she never knew what hurts and wounds she would encounter. The elixir wasn't like her other tinctures and tonics, salves and balms. She had to draw secretly on her little trickle of Faerie power to give it healing magic.

Oswin swung to face her, and Melly couldn't hide her flinch. The sheriff's guard had brawn he never hesitated to use. His habitual expression didn't invite friendliness, yet now he gave a gap-toothed smile. She still didn't like his piggy eyes.

"No pain," he gruffed. "Could use some of that m'self." He rolled his rounded shoulders then flexed his arms. "Came out the worst when I tussled with that wrestler from Lincoln."

She didn't succeed at hiding her grimace. Her power only worked when she shared with any who asked. She had prayed Oswin and his ilk never asked. As a healer for women, men normally spurned her help.

Oswin's interest in the elixir eclipsed his aversion about using his wife's healer.

"You oughta gimme it. I got hurts."

His *hurts* were scarcely on the same level as Jocine's broken bones. In the past, she'd dodged such requests with a pretense of arrogance. Wouldn't hurt to try that again. Melly lifted her chin and looked down her long, narrow nose. "I have liniment for sore muscles."

"I need treatment, woman. Round out the coins you keep costin' me."

Her temper rose. "Remember that cost next time, Oswin, before you break your wife's fingers. Or her arm. Or leave her face so battered that her eyes are swollen shut."

"She ain't no wife. Jest a woman."

Melly opened her mouth to argue, but Oswin wasn't worth it. When Jonice healed, Melly would repeat his words. Hopefully, they would be the crack in the wall of her devotion.

Oswin didn't often appear when Melly attended his wife. He'd remained this time. She didn't know the reason. That change worried her. Nottingham had been disrupted of late. Murmurs and complaints had reached Melly, who kept apart from most of the town's gossip. The rumors complained of the robbery of rich merchants traveling on the King's Road through Sherwood Forest.

In light of those rumors, maybe placating him was the right

thing to do.

"I have very little elixir remaining. It is rare and expensive." She reached for the scrip and closed her fingers tightly on the leather pouch.

He flexed stubby fingers. "You refusing a guard? The sheriff won't like that. Gimmie that pouch of yours."

"I'll get it." She hunted for a vial similar to the one that held the Fae-powered elixir.

He snapped forward and jerked the scrip out of her hands. He up-ended it and gave a shake.

Pouches of herbs, rolled bandages, prepared poultices, and stoppered clay pots landed on the dirt and scattered. The all-important magicked vials remained tucked in their slots. Oswin shook the scrip again. More simples dropped out, including a roll of linen. The cloth dropped and unfolded on the hard-packed dirt floor. Tiny glass vials winked out.

Oswin crouched and seized the linen roll. He tossed the scrip down.

Melly stretched out a hand then withdrew it. He would ignore anything she said. Whether she told truth or lied or gave a warning about poison, Oswin would not listen.

He stared at the vials. The liquids were vari-colored, one tinted yellow, another green. A third and more dangerous poison was colored like a cherry syrup. Oswin pulled out a yellow-tinted vial that resembled the one she had tucked away. He had watched her more closely than she had realized.

He popped the cork, sniffed and recoiled. "Stinks. I don't remember a stink."

"Please don't," she pleaded—but she omitted that he held a strong emetic.

He touched his tongue to the vial then spat the taste. "Blech! She didn't react when you gave her this. Tastes like poison."

"I diluted it. I used only a few drops in watered ale."

"Get me some ale."

With shaking hands, she turned to the table behind her. The cup she'd used with Jocine was there. She sloshed ale into it from a bottle. When she reached for water, he snapped, "Give it to me."

"A little water will dilute it."

"Don't need it. How much?"

She cleared her throat. *How can I stop him? What will he do to me?* "One drop." She tugged the scrip away from him and began gathering her simples and potions, her bandages and poultices.

He measured three drops of the emetic into the ale. That amount wouldn't kill him, but he would be in agony. When he returned the vial, she quickly stowed it. Then she backed away.

Oswin planted himself on the three-legged stool beside the hearth. "How long before it works?"

"Not long. You saw."

"I saw her fret then go to sleep."

"Aye, the hours of pain exhausted her." Melly swept her shawl around her shoulders. "I should be getting on."

"Go on then. Don't want to stare at your pinched face."

She slammed the rickety door, yet she hovered outside, unable to leave. Waiting.

But why wait? She knew what would happen. She knew how long he would spew and retch and heave long after his stomach emptied. One drop caused spewing for a candlemark. Three drops cleansed a system.

If she allowed him to suffer, her time in Nottingham was over. Defiance had never worked in previous towns, but placating also did not work.

Melly liked this town. For three years she'd had a good life. She'd avoided the sheriff's men and the town officials. She'd successfully hidden the magic that created her elixirs and balms. What Oswin called a pinched face, her sharp nose and chin and her angled cheekbones and eyes, were the only obvious signs of her Faerie blood, diluted over seven generations.

He retched. And did so again. Then he spewed the contents of his stomach. When he had a moment of ease, he cursed her and her healing, then he spewed again.

Melly opened the door and stepped inside. She stayed well back. The room stank of sickness. He was on hands and knees before the hearth, spitting.

"What did you give me, witch? Jocine didn't spew out her stomach. You tried to kill me."

"You chose the liquid, Oswin. You should have diluted it with ale and water. That prevents vomiting." *That wasn't quite a lie.*

He cursed her again. Then he grabbed his stomach and fought the emetic before he spewed liquid that stank of bile.

"I can stop it," she offered. "You'll sleep a bit and wake sore, nothing more. A small price."

He heaved though nothing emerged. "Gimme, witch. Gimme."

"Swear an oath for your attempted theft."

"Like Hell. You tried to kill me."

"You chose the liquid."

"You didn't say a word to stop me."

"Never cross a healer, Oswin. You must swear an oath— never say a word against me or of this business."

"Curse you, witch." Then he retched again. He fell forward, onto his hands, onto the sickness covering the dirt-packed floor. The emetic found liquid from somewhere and tossed it out of his throat.

She found the curative and waited until he dragged a hand over his dripping mouth. Then she offered the packet of dried herbs. "Swear, and I'll give you these."

"You want me dead."

"No. I want you to leave me alone."

"I'll never forget, witch."

"Good." She waved the packet. "Swear, Oswin. A simple oath. You will never say word against me or of this business."

He heaved. He swallowed mightily. Then he snatched the packet. "I swear. What do I do with this?"

"Say the words, Oswin, or the curative will not work." A deliberate lie, that. He had called her a witch. Let him think she had that power.

"I swear." Grudgingly he added, "Never a word spoken on this business."

Good enough. "Chew the leaves. Every sprig, every stem, every green bit. You will have time enough to clear this mess before the soporific takes effect."

He retched then tore open the packet and crammed leaves into his mouth. His red-rimmed eyes never left her. His shoulders and torso jolted with a dry heave.

"You must swallow."

He cursed her around the herbs, but he swallowed. She sloshed ale into the cup and offered it. He snatched it away and gulped it down. On his first breath after, he growled, "You'll pay."

"Remember your oath." She retreated to the door.

"Here, you! Clean this up."

"You made it. You clean it." Then she shut the door and hurried away.

Did I do enough to keep me safe here in Nottingham?

No. Oswin would plot a revenge.

She sighed. She had to leave. That meant buying a cart and a horse, packing up her little household, finding a leash for Rollo her hound, and taking once more to the road. Friends abandoned. Starting alone yet again.

Better to start her preparations tomorrow, on market day. That would also give her time to say farewell to Ellen and her friends.

No one stared at her swift walk through the town and the gates and along the road. She was a healer, often about on dire business.

Her hut came into view, tucked behind a grainfield. The little wooden building sheltered beneath tall oaks that dropped acorns into the thatch, where they tried to burrow in and sprout new trees every spring. Her herb garden, already harvested, dried in the fortnight's drought. Bunches of her harvest hung from beams in her main room, waiting transfer to the still room, once a shed. Her pottager garden had stopped producing. She should pick the last of the yield.

Then her hound bayed a halloo, tired of his few hours inside. And she smiled, knowing what she would do first.

Rollo knew better than to leap upon her, but he crowded her, his whole body wagging his excitement at her return. His sleek body showed scars from his old master before she'd rescued him and won his undying loyalty. He'd drunk his bowl dry. She fetched more water, and his lapping filled the hut.

Next thing she replenished her scrip, an old habit she never broke. Rollo followed her every step, across the room and back, in and out of the still room.

When satisfied with her work, she crossed the strap over her breast and picked up a heavy cloth pack. She knew a bramble patch where berries still fruited. Then she fetched the rope she used as a large harness. Rollo quivered at this sign of an explore. As soon as she opened the door, he hauled her out.

Melly laughed, her trouble with Oswin cast behind her. "Let me latch the door."

Rollo strained at the harness.

"You don't even know where we're going," she scolded. He whined. "Not town," she reassured him. When she turned him away from Nottingham, toward the fields and forest, he gave his two-note call. His eagerness nearly pulled her off her feet.

Far from Nottingham, she let the hound off the harness. He bounded away. She watched his joyful run with an uplifted heart.

His first energy expended, he headed back to where she picked berries from the bramble patch. He nosed along the verge between field and Sherwood Forest. When he ventured into the forest, she called him back. He always returned, looking both contrite and thwarted from following an intriguing scent.

They headed back, Melly dragging her heels, Rollo still exploring. The sun streaked vivid pinks and purples into the sky over Nottingham. The wind gusted through the trees and rippled like ocean waves across the grain.

She had no premonition, so the men standing outside her hut surprised her.

Guards, wearing the leathers and colors favored by the sheriff.

A sinking gloom predicted that Oswin had broken his oath.

She could run. The guards had not yet spotted her.

Yet even as she formed the thought, a guard spied her. He shouted to his fellows. More emerged from inside her hut.

She drew nearer but stopped at her withy gate. Rollo sensed her wariness. He growled at the two men who neared.

A captain, she saw. The other she didn't know. "You come with us," the captain demanded.

Through the harness rope, Rollo sensed her fear. He resumed growling.

"Captain, am I charged?" she asked, trying for a reasonable tone. "What is the complaint against me? Who made it?"

"Never you mind," the other man said.

"Shut it, Berne. I'm doing this." The captain scowled at her. "Keep your hands where I can see them. Charge is poison. Oswin's woman says you tried to kill him."

"Jocine said that?"

"You poisoned him. He was sick all over their home. She had to fetch the physick to him. At first, he couldn't stay awake. Roused enough to tell her what happened."

"But he lives," Berne crowed. "You failed. He'll see you in gaol."

"I didn't poison him. I had no reason to."

"Don't matter," the captain said and opened the gate. "You're coming with us."

The hound crouched and snarled, sounding like a vicious animal.

"Call off the dog," the captain ordered.

She released the rope harness.

Rollo sprang for the captain. The man fell back into Berne. They tangled together on the ground.

The guards behind them reacted too late. Blocked by their captain and Berne, they couldn't get through the gate. Nor could they climb over her withy fence. Tall enough to keep out deer, the withy fence would break under their weight.

"Rollo! Come!"

He stopped worrying the captain and looked sheepish.

As soon as Melly had the hound's attention, she ran, lifting her skirts high so nothing hindered her long legs. The scrip and pack bounced against her. Rollo bounded beside her, all eagerness to run.

The guards yelled. They would follow.

She wished—oh, she wished … *but could I have changed anything?* Jocine had needed help. Oswin chose to drink the emetic. Would he have stopped if she warned him?

The shouts drew closer.

Melly plunged into the forest at the first path she saw. Rollo stayed on her heels. The guards were not far behind.

The path ran clear and wide, a straight trail with no

encroaching branches or bushes. The hound kept pace, darting forward a few times, dropping back to investigate a smell. Only once did she need to call Rollo to her. Good hound that he was, he leaped to her, tongue lolling out of his square muzzle.

When she slowed, not able to maintain a full-out run for long. Rollo didn't slow, just deepened his ventures before and behind. Melly saw a narrow deer track, and she veered off the wide trail onto it. The hound followed. The underbrush encroached on this trail. Brambles caught her skirt. Shafts of sunlight came fewer, farther apart as ancient thick-trunked trees replaced the younger ones growing at the forest's perimeter. She chased side trail after side trail, hoping to lose her pursuers in the maze.

The guards shouted less, but they still crashed along. They had fallen behind. She hoped they had missed the turn onto the new path.

The new trail remained constant. She ran until she stumbled and fell. The hound jumped over her, around her, thinking it a game. Her chest heaved with her gusting breath. She pushed Rollo off and scrambled up.

The trees revealed no guards. No shouts came, yet very faint was a determined crashing. A few guards must still trail her.

Her troubles in other towns had never come from the authorities. Oswin's poisoning would turn the whole barracks against her. That he'd stolen the emetic to drink, that she'd not caused his poisoning, that she'd never given trouble in her three years in Nottingham, that she provided a needed service to the women and the poor—none of that would matter.

Walking slowly, working to slow her breath, Melly considered her situation. She had wanted a quiet life in Nottingham. She sighed at a crash far behind. Telling distance in a forest was difficult. Her little bit of Faerie heritage sharpened her senses—never enough to match the Faer folk, never enough to reveal her blood.

That would get her burned as a witch.

As Oswin had accused.

She could never return to Nottingham.

Twilight was coming. The dimness under the trees had already deepened. How long would the guards follow her? She had no idea where in the forest she was, not even a direction.

But she had Rollo and long experience at being resourceful. She'd started from scratch before. She could do it again.

Rollo followed his nose along another path, and Melly followed him.

.~.~.~.

The low fire burned inside a stony circle. Melly hoped the flames kept away the four-legged predators. She knew wolves still roamed the forest, no matter what others claimed. She hoped that she'd lost her two-legged predators.

Rollo crowded against her, lifting his cold muzzle to her fingers. He'd eaten well on forest hare. He had spooked it as twilight became darkness. The foolish thing had leaped onto the trail and soon died, and Melly winced as she compared the death to the events of her day. She had berries and nuts and water, a better repast than she would have received in gaol.

Giant beeches encircled the clearing. She had gathered fuel to last till morning. A small fire shouldn't alert the searchers. Fortune favored her, for they were into autumn but this night had no scent of morning frost. With the fire on one side and Rollo on the other, she would stay warm.

She woke to Rollo growling.

She blinked hazily. Blackness surrounded the camp. The forest had a waiting stillness. Something lurked near.

Rollo wasn't barking, so it wasn't a predator. Had the guards found her? Yet whatever came didn't crash as it pushed through the underbrush.

The hound sprang to his feet. He faced away from the trail that had brought them to this clearing. His whole body quivered with excitement.

Melly fed more fuel to the fire. The flames leapt higher, lighting the clearing.

Then three black hounds streamed into the space.

They began as slender shadows slinking from the forest into the grassy clearing. Like sooty smoke, they expanded in size. Black as the night, narrow of muzzle, sleek and long-legged. Fire gleamed on their coats. Their eyes glowed red.

Melly gasped. Faerie hounds, vicious to their prey.

Rollo whined with eagerness.

A black hound came near. The dogs met in the way of dogs, muzzles touching, sniffing along bodies. The Faer hound seemed friendly—although a single snap would kill the smaller dog.

Moving slowly, Melly climbed to her feet.

The black hounds froze and snarled. Rollo, engaged in exploratory sniffs, ignored her. When she stood still, fingers grasping her skirts, the three hounds returned to greeting her dog. She stared at the blackness from which they'd emerged. Did more fiery eyes watch the camp? Did the blackness move?

One of the three came to her, sniffing, freezing her hand with its icy muzzle. Then the other two came. Still moving carefully, she rubbed the back of her hand over the hounds' heads. Rollo crowded in as the hounds pressed close, and she staggered a step. "Pretty boys. Aren't you sweet?"

A hound bumped hard, and she staggered again, but she had advanced to caressing their slender skulls, their silky ears.

Then a fifth head imposed, asking for petting, and she realized three more hounds had joined the twisting, tangling circle around her.

Six Faerie hounds, black as night, eyes red as coals, cold and beautiful, savage hunters who jostled around her, wanting attention.

Movement beyond them caught her eye. Shrouded in black, a figure stepped from the trees.

He shed shadows as he neared the fire.

Faerie. Tall. Dressed in hunter's leather. Steel glinted firelight, sword hilts, knife hilts. As the shadows released him, she saw angled features, pale skin and black eyes, a mouth shaped into an upside down peak.

He wore an antler crown. His silver-flax hair fell in a shimmering cascade.

He spoke Faer, words she didn't recognize, and the six hounds left her. Tail wagging, Rollo pranced to meet the Faerie huntsman.

The man bent and ran long fingers over her hound's head. He found a spot and rubbed, and Rollo melted against him. He flopped at the Faerie's feet, content until another new thing caught his attention.

The black hounds stationed themselves around the clearing.

The huntsman stretched a hand toward her. Sparkling light surrounded her then compressed. Melly cried out in startlement then could not get breath for another cry as magic squeezed life from her.

Rollo sensed her distress. He leaped to her side and whined. Then he bumped her. When she couldn't respond to him, he turned to snarl at the Faerie. When that had no effect on her suffering, Rollo growled then barked, demanding. He hunched, prepared to leap to her defense. The Wild Hunt hounds would destroy him before he neared the Faerie. Melly could do nothing, suspended in that light with its increasing compression. She feared for her hound.

The huntsman dropped his hand. The dangerous light disappeared. She dragged in grateful breaths then knelt to reward Rollo with pats and tugging on his ears. His tail wagged fiercely, beating her side. He licked her face, doggie kisses.

"No, no, Rollo," she dodged. He gave a happy whine, nosed her again then pranced back to the huntsman, sure of his welcome. He crouched at the Faerie's feet, tongue lolling, tail still wagging, looking hopeful.

The huntsman laughed and rewarded Rollo with a tidbit. The hound crunched it happily then flopped at his feet.

Melly straightened, trying to stand taller. Meeting the huntsman's eyes set her aquiver with fear. She dropped into a deep curtsey. "My lord Cerne," she murmured. She rose, keeping her gaze lowered.

"Lovely lady, what brings you into our forest?" That deep voice reverberated to her bones.

Our forest. Had she offended an unknown Fae law? "Forgive, my lord, any offense. I did not intend—."

He chuffed a laugh. "Fear not, lovely lady. What brings you here? You are far inside our bright forest. From whence come you?"

"Nottingham, my lord."

He advanced. Rollo came at his heels.

The black hounds encircled her again, distracting her. Their red eyes gleamed. One pressed close and snarled. She presented a fist. The hound sniffed then nudged her hand. She petted and scratched behind ears. Another crowded close, then all were there, clamoring for attention.

She risked a glance at the huntsman. He no longer looked the scary leader of the Wild Hunt. Watching his hounds, he looked like any indulgent owner.

They pushed at her, and she staggered. Not wanting to fall, she crouched. A mistake, for they were great in size, stronger than she. The mass of them could easily overwhelm her. They sensed her fear and growled, but she continued giving pats, accepted their nudges, hoping she didn't land on her back, like easy prey.

"My hounds approve." The huntsman snapped his fingers, and the hounds left her again, dispersing around the clearing. One stayed close, inches between them.

When he waved his hand, the flames leaped, brightening her view of him. "Please, lovely lady, sit by the fire. You shiver."

Not with cold. She didn't want him to loom over her, but she shifted to her former spot. Then he lithely lowered himself.

His gaze coursed around the clearing, landing on Rollo still gnawing at his tidbit. The Faerie's expression changed briefly, how she could not say, then he stared at her, as close an examination as he must have indulged in when he watched from the forest.

"The scars on your hound, you did not cause them?"

"No. I healed Rollo. Then I bought him from his cruel master."

"Coins," he scoffed. He shocked her then, for he lifted off the antler crown and rested it on his bent leg. "You have Faer blood, lovely lady."

"A weak stream," she admitted, "from years upon years ago. My grandmother's grandmother's grandmother."

"Seven generations you are. Of what name are you?"

"Melisandre, my lord, but my friends call me Melly."

That peaky smile deepened. "Am I a friend?"

"My lord—."

"You know my name," he interrupted.

Her heart started racing again.

He chuffed another laugh. "Do you fear me, Melly of Nottingham? Or do you fear the men who hunt you more?"

She had no reply to that.

"You know who I am. You know I seek and punish those who commit evil."

"Those men—they followed me this deeply into the forest?"

"They are far enough not to see your fire, but they hunt you. I came to meet their prey."

She fought strangled words past the constriction in her throat. "You are the huntsman. These are the hounds of the Wild Hunt. And I am no longer of Nottingham. I have ... left there."

"The reason you are in our forest? You have few possessions." His gaze fastened on her scrip. "Healing herbs and poisons."

Melly winced. "Aye, my lord Cerne."

"Those poisons—one of those who hunts you reeks of a poison of yours."

Oswin. She could swear the emetic and curative would have prevented his following her. Berne had even said Oswin was at the gaol, waiting for her to be charged. "He stole it from me and drank it, not knowing it would sicken him. He thought it was the pain soother that I had given his wife."

"A fool then. And the other man?"

"Another guard. I suppose—his friend Berne?"

"These two drove you from Nottingham and into our forest?"

"Basically, aye, Lord Cerne."

"Have you ever poisoned anyone deliberately, Melly of Nottingham?"

Is that a trick question? "Only in necessity."

"What do you call necessity?" Curiosity colored his voice.

"I have never murdered anyone. At times poison can help a sickness. If they have eaten or drunk a greater poison, mine may save their life. That is rare. I don't seek to use the poisons, but I would be a fool not to have them in my stock, my lord."

"And you are not a fool. You use them rarely?"

"Rarely and only when I fear for life."

"Do others approach you for poisons?"

"They have," she admitted faintly, and he scowled fiercely. Danger emanated from him. Two of the black hounds growled, savage and fearsome.

"You humans like your coin," he disparaged. "Did you live in luxury after you helped kill?"

"I refused to sell. I refused to be their means of murder."

His frown cleared. "And they accepted that?"

"One time, no. I must move once anyone discovers that I have poisons."

"You never sell your poisons? But I think some humans have stolen from you."

"Unfortunately, my lord."

"And you moved on?"

"I could not stay. Someone has to be blamed for the death," she admitted bitterly.

"Human laws do not always serve justice, is that not true? Even though you did not administer the poison. And these men who hunt you, Melly of Nottingham? Why do they pursue you so deeply into our bright forest?"

"Revenge. To punish me."

"Or to take the poisons from you? Sell them to others who want to murder? Commit murder themselves? This could be their plan. What will you do when they capture you?"

She huffed. "I do not intend for them to capture me."

He laughed, no longer looking a stern huntsman. "No, they should not capture a lovely lady who has a trickle of Faer blood. That would offend me." He stood, a blur in her sight. The antler crown was restored to his head though she'd not seen the movement. The hounds leaped to stand beside him—and Rollo, eager, pressing against the huntsman's legs. "Sleep, Lady Melisandre. I will return ere dawn. Stay with your mistress," he ordered Rollo. "Dubh, Fekete, Eldur, remain here." Then he turned, three hounds with him, and night swallowed them.

Rollo came to Melly, wagging and nudging, chilling her neck with his wet nose. She let him climb into her lap. The other Hunt hounds remained near, watching.

She didn't think they would attack.

As the flames died back to the smoldering fire of earlier, she wondered over that strange conversation. Soon, though, Melly yawned and gave in to the Faerie's instruction that she sleep. The ground had cooled. She would have shivered, but Rollo pressed his warmth alongside her.

The other hounds sprawled at her feet.

She slept immediately. She didn't dream.

When she woke this time, night still cloaked the clearing. In the sky, stars twinkled, a light path across the heavens. Rollo slept beside her. The black hounds stood at her feet. They stared into the forest. One turned to look when she sat up. His eyes pulsed red.

Then she heard screams, not near. Not far. Gradually muffled.

She shuddered, her fears about Cerne's disappearance confirmed.

Had he hunted the guards because she had a trickle of Faer blood remaining to her?

Or as punishment for pursuing her into Sherwood, *our forest*?

She didn't—couldn't sleep. Cerne's return terrified her. What price would he exact?

Will he consider me bound to him now?

She paced the clearing. One hound, sometimes all three trailed her. The stars spun away, and the sky lightened, the first herald of dawn.

Cerne came then, striding out of the forest, the three hounds at his heels, eyes burning, tongues lolling.

Rollo woke then and rushed to join the hounds welcoming their master's return.

The fire leaped, offering warmth that didn't reach her icy chill.

She forced herself to meet those black, black eyes. "My lord Cerne—." The words clung to her throat.

He anticipated her question. "They live, but they no longer search for you, Lady Melisandre."

"What did—may I ask what you did with them?"

He bowed his antlered head. "They visit Underhill. My cousin the duchess sets them to a redeeming task. They will never again threaten you." His gaze pinned her. "What is your will? Will you remain in our bright forest or return to Nottingham?"

A third option? But he offered none, and she feared to ask. Cerne was a dread Faerie lord. Melly considered ways to answer him and settled for "I will not return. All my possessions are there, but I need them not."

His mouth quirked, once again offering that peaky smile that had tricked her into thinking he was—not safe, just not mercurial and totally strange. He tilted his head. A strange look flashed. "I have friends, mortal friends, who will help you." He extended his hand. "Come, lovely lady. Meet my friends."

She caught up her scrip and pack then dared to accept his clasp. His hand was warmer than hers. She firmed her grip. *Never*, her grandmother had warned, *never show weakness to the Faer folk.*

"Never fear with me, lovely lady." As he spoke, shadows swallowed them, the hounds, and Rollo.

They emerged to a warmer darkness, with a fire and three groggy men, two with hair bright as the flames.

The men didn't react to their appearance until the hounds rushed to greet them. One held back, smaller in size, but two men welcomed the hounds as old friends.

When Rollo asked for his share of the pets and scratches, a man exclaimed, "What's this? A mortal dog?"

"The hound of the lady Melisandre," Cerne said and drew her from the shadows. The three leapt to their feet. He guided her to the fireside. He didn't release her hand. Melly didn't know when her terror had abated to nothingness. "She joins your camp in our bright forest. You will call her Melly, and she retains my shield."

Melly had a better look at the slight one, tall boy yet still a boy. "Tod!"

The boy gaped. "Is it—Melly? It is! What are you doing here in Sherwood?"

"This boy is a friend?" Cerne asked. "The duchess remembers him fondly."

She stared up at him, those black eyes, the angled cheekbones and eyebrows that made him strange, and the peaky smile that gave him warmth. "It's Tod. We—Ellen and I wondered what had happened to him."

"I found Robin Hood's men," the boy interjected. "We live here in Sherwood. We work against the sheriff."

The last excited him, and Melly's gaze swept the other two men, wondering that they let a mere boy join their fight against the sheriff.

Her look prompted Tod to introduce them. "This is Will Scarlet, and this is Much of Muchness."

"Welcome," the shorter one said. "Anyone that Lord Cerne brings is welcome here."

The huntsman's clasp tightened. He looked at the brightening sky, pink already tinging the clouds. "Lady Melisandre, you will remain here. I must depart. I will come to you on the full of the moon." He lifted her hand. His lips grazed her roughened knuckles.

"My lord," she murmured.

He released her and stepped back. Head lifted high, he spoke to the hounds, those strange words of earlier. They streamed past him. Shadows grew dense, and they raced into the darkness. When he strode away, Melly felt curiously bereft. A strange feeling, for how could she feel forlorn about the huntsman's leaving when he had nearly killed her and when his hunting of the guards had frightened her?

Will Scarlet, Tod tagging at his heels, escorted her to a hut. Tod proudly said that he was standing watch and would see her later. Before the morning brightened, she found herself on a pallet, Rollo with her, and sleep pressing heavily.

The camp at noon was lively. A hot stew filled her, and Rollo gnawed happily at bones. Tod eagerly recounted his adventures. Then she was led to the edge of the camp, where a man perched on an exposed boulder. "Robin Hood," Tod whispered loudly.

With light brown hair and a slender form, he scarcely looked strong enough to stand against a breeze, let alone the sheriff of Nottingham. Then she spied the fierceness in those blue eyes, lit by an inner fire. When Melly curtsied, he looked disconcerted. "No, no, we are all equals here." Then he ruined that by adding, "Lady Melisandre."

"It's Melly," she told him, "and I'm far from a lady."

"Melly it is," he agreed. "Do you wish to travel on or stay with us?"

"I'm a healer." Boldly she added, "Since you're fighting the sheriff, you can use my skills."

A man popped up on the other side of the boulder. Tall, very tall, with a thick black beard and disconcertingly green eyes. "I hear you're a poisoner, too."

"That's Little John," Tod hissed.

"Not a poisoner," she retorted. "A healer."

"And a friend of Faeries," Robin added. "Healer and Faerie friend. Doubly welcome to our camp, Melly."

Three Yule Feasts for the Faeries

The stew had simmered all afternoon, and its aroma filled the hut. Ellen sniffed happily as she sliced a loaf that hadn't sold at today's market.

She'd given away other unsold loaves to her friends and to street urchins rather than carry everything back to her hut. The bread would only turn stale.

Butter on the table, watered ale in a mug, she gave one last stir to the stew before she fetched a bowl from the top shelf over her workboard.

A sharp knock rapped on her door.

Who could be visiting so late? Even with the shortened days, the night was well advanced. Most would be retired for the night. Ellen's late start on supper had pushed back her one meal of the day.

She'd taken over the hut after Melly disappeared. Located beyond Nottingham's walls, it was tucked against Sherwood Forest. Seeing light through the ill-fitted shutters, did someone hope the healer had returned? Or had a guard decided to investigate? Melly fled into the forest when accused of poison. Two guards pursued her. None of them returned. Could it be—?

The knock repeated, insistent.

Ellen set down the bowl and picked up her butcher knife. When she opened the door, no one stood without. Then, by the withy gate, she saw movement. She clutched the knife more tightly.

A man approached. Darkness slipped off him, as if shadows slithered away. Pale, pale skin. A shimmering cascade of silver hair. Sharp features. The sword at his hip glinted although the racing clouds hid the moon.

Faerie.

She fell back from the door as he gained the threshold. And he smiled, a curious upside-down peak. *Does my retreat amuse him?* The door flapped shut, enclosing them in the single room.

"Well met, lady." He gave a single nod.

Ellen retreated to place the table between them. Meeting his courtesy with the threat of the knife embarrassed her. She dropped the knife beside the bread loaf.

He glanced at the bread and butter, the cup of ale, the empty bowl. "I interrupt your repast. My apologies, lady."

She cleared her throat. "My lord, no apology is necessary." Only then did she remember to drop a curtsey. She deepened it, offering the courtesy due to an earl rather a baron, and she hoped this Faerie knew the difference.

His smile deepened then vanished. His face was wondrous strange, with its angled brow and cheekbones, the sharp nose and chin, the peaky smile. He wore leathers, like a ranger, fitted close to his tall, lean body. He leaned his bow against the door jamb. She glimpsed yellow-fletched arrows in his quiver. Knife hilts winked at his waist and tucked in his tall boots, and a fifth slid in the scabbard sewn onto the leather baldric that crossed his chest. "I come on a mission, lady."

"A mission?"

"Is this the abode of Lady Melisandre?"

"Lady Melisandre?" she echoed. How could this hut with its rickety door and shutters and the patched walls that admitted every gust of wind be the abode of a lady? Then her mind started working through her shock. "Oh, you mean Melly?"

"Aye, that is a name I have heard associated with her."

"You know Melly? Melisandre? Is she unhurt? Safe? She disappeared when the guards tried to arrest her. What happened?" Ellen stopped peppering him with questions. Little though she knew of Faeries, she doubted they liked questions. "My apologies, my lord. May I offer you ale?"

His expression lightened although she would not have said that he had frowned. He gave an appreciative sniff. "I am intrigued by this aroma. Boar I recognize, but the other smells escape me."

"Pig, actually. We are forbidden to hunt boar. It's naught but stew with a few spices. Would you like a bowlful?" she dared.

"I hunger, but I would not take the food from your mouth, lady."

"I have extra. I made too much." Just a bit too much, but this Faerie didn't need to know that. She would share. Even with what she'd given away, she had enough bread to fill her belly for days.

"I have a yearning to taste this human food."

Human. The word interrupted her in mid-pour of ale. She continued pouring, hoping he hadn't noticed her pause. She set the cup opposite her seat, across from her own watered ale. "Please, my lord, sit you down."

He looked askance at her ale cup.

"That is the better chair," she defended.

He gave a short laugh. "You honor me, lady."

"It's not lady. Plain Ellen Best. That's good enough for the likes of me."

"Then, you honor me, Plain Ellen Best."

Is he mocking me? She set out two clay plates then picked up the bowl intended for herself and ladled it full of stew. When she placed it before him, he leaned over it and inhaled deeply.

She ladled her own stew. As she came around the table, he asked. "How does one eat this?"

"I forgot." Because he flustered her. Kicking herself mentally, she backed up to her workboard and brought back two spoons. She sliced more bread as he examined the tin utensil. She winced, thinking he must dine with silver and crystal. Luckily for her embarrassment, he said nothing. She served him three slices of bread, one to herself, then took her chair.

He had waited. When she dipped her spoon into the stew, he asked, "Are there not words that humans say before a meal?"

"Words? You mean 'grace'? A prayer to God, to thank Him for our food and to ask for His blessings upon us."

"Grace. Do you not say these words?"

She looked at her spoon. The stew still steamed. "I don't. It's just me." *Foolish*, she chided, *telling a Faerie that I live alone.* "Bless this food. Let our nourish our bodies. Thank you, God our Father." Then she took her first bite, grateful that her empty stomach hadn't betrayed her. Ellen took several bites before she realized that each of his followed hers, stew or bread.

He grimaced at the ale. "What is *this?*"

"Ale. It's like beer. Have you ever—what do you usually drink?"

"Wine."

"Ah. This is far from that."

He nodded firmly. "You made this?"

"I bought it from one of the taverns, the Tinker's Wife." She didn't share that the tavern was the cheapest in Nottingham.

He hovered his hand over the ale. Sparkles twinkled under his palm and dropped into the ale. When they ended, he motioned. "I would deal with your cup."

She passed it over. "What are you doing?"

"Your drink should be worthy of this meal." Magic glittered its way into her pint. He offered it to her. "Drink." Then he held his hand over the flagon.

She sipped. Wine, a wine so fine of flavor that she took a greater swallow. Not even when she'd stolen a sip while working in a baron's kitchen had the wine been so wonderful, like nectar rather than an acidic fermentation. "Oh my."

He beamed.

"I'm ashamed I gave you that ale. Thank you for—well, the magic."

"A simple transference. Two in Underhill are now drinking ale."

"You switched—?" She giggled then clapped a hand over her mouth. "They won't be happy."

He held out his empty bowl. "Is there more?"

The Faerie's appetite dwarfed hers, and he finished the stew she'd intended to eat for the morrow as well as all the bread on the table. He looked longingly at the other loaves on her workboard, but Ellen didn't offer them. She needed to eat something to tide her over the next days, and a single egg from hens that despised the cold would only go so far.

She did have one thing to offer, a fresh nut and dried apple flatbread, sweetened with honey. She grated cinnamon and nutmeg from her carefully guarded stock. She also offered her hunk of cheddar, a bit of salt to offset the sweet.

"What is this?"

"Try it. Tell me what you think."

He scarfed up the flatbread but ignored the cheese. Then he leaned back. "You have given me quite a feast, Plain Ellen Best. You did not hesitate to share your bounty with me, a Faerie and a stranger."

She turned from setting his empty bowl in the dry sink. "I am rewarded when people enjoy my cooking. You certainly did."

"I have a proposition for you. A bargain if you will."

Never bargain with Faeries. How many times had she heard that? *Never show weakness to a Faerie.* Would refusing be construed as a weakness?

Yet how did she reject a Faerie bargain without causing offense? "What kind of bargain?" she asked cautiously.

"You have given me a feast of your plain fare, Plain Ellen Best, and you shall be rewarded. I propose two more feasts, a fine dinner for my friends, and then a Yule feast for an honored guest."

The bargain appalled her. "You want me to cook for Faeries?" The dangers, the mortal risks, the real fear of a failed dinner—everything that could go wrong snatched her breath away. How to refuse? "I don't have the stock. My pantry—."

"What you need will be provided. Would you do this? Will aught interfere?"

No one had hired her for their Yuletide feasts; she couldn't use that excuse. No one bought her breads and pasties at market; they saved their pennies to afford special holiday treats. She could devote all her time and energies to this.

"Two more feasts?" she confirmed.

"Coppers for this one, silvers for the next, gold for the third. I know how you mortals crave the coins."

In her younger days, Ellen had known the folly of craving coins. Since then, she'd traveled paths sinful and harmful, paths that left scars on her soul and her memories and her body. Nottingham had given her a refuge. The new sheriff threatened some of that refuge.

A few coins would keep her this winter. Silvers would fund her departure. She didn't want to leave the town. Coins, though, gave her the option if things went wrong. God knew, she'd had a lot to go wrong. And no one knew all that was stored in Melly's root cellar or how to access it. Certainly not the guards who had wrecked the hut after Melly disappeared.

"Do you accept the bargain, Plain Ellen Best?"

"Let me think. Tell me about the mission that brought you here."

"Aye, a favor to my friend Lord Cerne. He can answer your questions about Lady Melisandre, whom you call Melly. You may ask him at the next dinner. The third feast, your final one, will be an elaborate dinner for someone of great importance. You would do these?"

"What's this favor for Lord Cerne?"

He smiled, that curious upside-down vee that gave him an impish look as if her counter-point pleased him. "The favor to my lord Cerne is to collect the possessions of Lady Melisandre."

"The possessions—?" *What does a Faerie want with Melly's things? Unless he intends to restore them to her.* That gave her hope for her friend. Wherever Melly was, she lived.

Ellen had mingled her possessions with Melly's and stowed away her clothes. "I will need time to sort them."

"The lady was most concerned for her herbs. When I bring the venison, I will collect those things."

"Venison?"

"The meat for the next feast. You have cooked venison in the past?"

Venison was another meat denied to commoners who had no funds to pay for a hunting tithe in the forest. "I have, when I cooked for a baron."

"I look forward to the dinner you will prepare." He stood, adjusting his scabbard. "You agree to this bargain, Plain Ellen Best?"

"I do not even know your name, my lord."

"Fenric. I am no lord, merely a sentinel for her grace."

No matter what could and would go wrong, Ellen wanted no mischievous or malicious Faerie with a grudge against her. She sidestepped a direct answer. "I will have Melly's herbs and winter clothes sorted when you bring the venison. I will need a full day to prepare the meat."

He picked up his glistening bow. "Expect me before the New Moon, Plain Ellen."

She followed him to the door, delving her memory for recipes that would enhance the venison. Definitely not stew and bread. He'd said feast, not dinner. Had she coin, she would purchase pewter bowls and plates, spoons and knives, goblets worthy of the name. "Will we have more of that wonderful wine?"

"You already do." On that cryptic answer, he left the hut.

Shadows gathered as he walked to the withy gate. The light streaming through the doorway reached that far, yet not seven paces from the door, darkness concealed him.

What have I gotten myself into?

Two more feasts. With Faeries, known for their discernment.

Although this Faerie, this Fenric, he had seemed easily pleased.

Ellen barred the door. That precaution was useless when a good axe swing or solid kick would take the rickety boards apart.

Then a strange twinkling caught her attention. She turned slowly.

Centered on the table, sparkling lights swirling above, was a pouch. Deerskin, thin and malleable, soft to the touch. The sparks flickered away when she picked up the pouch. They flitted around the room before winking out. The pouch had heft and chinked. Her fingers tingled. She untied the thong and peeked in. Coins. She spilled them onto the table. Copper coins. Foreign. Old. Not used in England. She would have to visit the moneychanger or a well-traveled merchant ... like the spice merchant. He would take them.

And spices would elevate her dishes. Spice and sweet.

She needed more honey. A hard block of sugar, highly expensive—but this abundance of coins now set it within her reach.

Hopefully, people would merely think she prepared a feast for a wealthy merchant or a baron. She need not name anyone.

After she hid the coins, she cleared the supper ... and began to plan.

.~.~.~.

No moon would rise tonight. The snow clouds hung heavy and thick after the day's dusting. The wind gusted, sweeping the world clean for the winter solstice next week.

A deer haunch roasted, a slow cook that kept the meat tender. It had miraculously appeared yesterday evening when she returned from market. The two sacks for Melly, bundled inside heavy blankets and wrapped with cords, had vanished.

The surprise with the venison was the leather bucket overflowing with blackberries. The season for berries had long since passed in the mortal world. These must be from the Faer land. They cooked like normal blackberries. After she began the roast, she had to hurry into Nottingham to buy vinegar, for the wine in her flagon stayed fresh, renewed every time she emptied and washed the jug.

Most of the blackberries spent the rest of the day steeping with cinnamon and thinned honey in watered vinegar. She also created a preserve for later in the winter when she craved something sweet. A small pumpkin gourd from last week's market had turned into four pies, flavored with cinnamon, nutmeg, ginger, and honey. She'd hidden the pies on a lower shelf and covered them with a cloth. Chopped parsnips and cut-off cooked portions of the deer haunch would create a pastry-covered dish. Salt and butter completed the slow roast in a small pot tucked into the coals. Last of all, she sauteed bitter greens and dried wild allium, harvested from a protected corner of Melly's garden.

Ellen was tapping the bottom of a round loaf of bread when the hut's door flew open. She slid the loaf onto her workboard. She hadn't even turned when a slight form flung arms around her.

"Best Cook! Best Cook!" called the voice muffled in her plump bosom.

"Tod?" She cautiously returned the hug. "Let me look at you. You can't have grown? You have!" She ran fingers through his fox-red hair.

The boy chortled and spread his arms wide. "Will says I grow too fast." He showed a leg with its raggedly cut hem well above short boots. "Look! Last time I saw you, these fit."

"You need new breeches." She said the obvious, hoping the

not-obvious news of his father would not be asked. Last heard, guards hauled all the prisoners in Nottingham Castle to the Assizes for judgment. Ellen prayed the boy didn't ask for specifics.

"Ellen!" Another rush before she expected it, more arms flung about her.

"Melly!" Ellen extracted her arms and returned her friend's embrace. "I was so afraid you were injured or worse. The Faerie told me enough to guess you were alive."

"I'm glad to see you're not living inside the walls. Nottingham's dangerous." She patted Ellen then stepped back. "You'll have better chances outside town. The friend of my lord Cerne said that Plain Ellen Best had taken my hut. That's better than it falling to ruin." She glanced around. "You've worked hard to improve it."

"I've had no time at all to work on it."

"But I saw no chinks of light coming through the walls. This hut was always so drafty, I dreaded winter. But the wind is not coming in. You're cozy here."

Ellen remembered the sparkling lights that flickered around, but she doubted that answer would serve. "Well, I've done nothing except prepare for tonight's feast."

"Tod and I are eager to try everything. We know you are Nottingham's best cook!"

Looking longingly at the round loaf, the boy chomped on a handful of nuts found on her workboard. "I miss your bread, Ellen. What all did you cook?"

"Venison and vegetables. Where are you two living? I hear nothing of you in town."

Melly snickered. "And you will not. We're in Sherwood."

"Sherwood! But there's outlaws and thieves—!"

Both laughed. "They may be outlaws," Melly admitted, "but they are good to us."

"They have to be," Tod added, "if they don't want to anger

Lord Cerne."

"Lord Cerne?"

"Oh, Ellen, I've so much to tell you," but before she launched into her news, two men came inside. Melly whispered, "No time for that now. You'll see."

The two men were Faeries. Fenric set his bow beside the door, the same place as before. The other Faerie overtopped him by a head. He had on similar dark hunting leathers. An imposing figure, he would have looked masculine even in embroidered silks and ermine.

Fenric bowed to her. "Fair evening, Ellen Best. May I present my lord Cerne?"

She froze in the midst of her curtsey as her mind identified the name. Cerne was the dreaded leader of the Wild Hunt with its hounds from blackest hell. And Fenric had called him friend. Neither Melly nor Tod looked frightened by his presence. "My lord," she murmured then shot a frown at Fenric. How could he not tell her that he would bring the lord of the Wild Hunt to this Yule feast?

Who would come to the next? *Her grace*, he had said. A Faerie duchess.

"Please, sit at the table." She indicated the three chairs and the long bench, two more purchases with the copper coins, exchanged for silver to pay the carpenter.

She poured wine, remembering to water Tod's, then brought the magicked clay jug so they could pour refills for themselves.

Fenric hadn't taken a chair. He followed her to the hearth. "Sit," she insisted.

"I am host. I will serve what you give me." Then he also wanted her to join the group around the table. She shared the bench with Tod.

As the feast progressed, Ellen could discern no complaints from either Faerie. Melly and she had one serving and were stuffed; Tod had two and belched with a youth's delight. The two

Faerie polished off the deer haunch, exclaimed over the blackberry sauce and the vegetables, and polished off three pies. Tod watched that display in awe.

Melly spoke of her new life. Ellen longed for it even as she couldn't see it working for her. A cook needed a hearth and an oven. Those couldn't be moved in the twinkling of an eye, needed when the rangers wandered close to Robin Hood's camp.

Ellen sensed emotions between Melly and Cerne, simmering slow, not quite ready to taste.

Tod was full of adventures, and the names Will and Jack and Much dropped readily from his lips. The one sad and awkward moment came when he shared, solemn and quiet, that his pa had not yet come before the judges of the Assizes.

The baying of a pack of hunting hounds ended their evening. Lord Cerne stood. He touched a curl of Melly's unbound hair. "The hounds grow restless, and I am remiss. Fenric will see you and Tod safely."

Melly insisted on helping Ellen clean. Tod fell asleep. The Faerie sentinel sharpened his sword and knives, two needle-thin, two jagged sharp, one blunt and broad, all glistening with magic.

Dawn crept in as they finished.

"Will you not stay?" Ellen asked. "We have scarce touched your time away. How is Rollo? Do you need anything? More clothes? Anything else from your stillroom?"

"I have what I need. Bundle up, Tod. It's snowing again."

"Lady Melisandre," Fenric said, his first words in hours, "sunrise approaches. We must depart."

Ellen was not surprised when she turned from barring the door to find another leather pouch on the table she'd just scrubbed, more lights twinkling about the hut.

Silver coins. All sizes and weights. Good English coins. She could spend these without trouble.

. ~ . ~ . ~ .

Fenric came three nights later. She had gone to add cooking scraps to her compost and returned to him sitting at the table, helping himself to her wine.

His wine, she admitted.

"I came to share your food and wine, Plain Ellen Best."

Ellen could only offer another simple repast that the Faerie must find poor fare after the ambrosia and nectar of the Faerie land. Fenric talked of the other evening, finishing with "My lord Cerne and his lady were well pleased."

And you? she wondered. "It was lovely to see Melly and Tod again. A happy surprise."

"You miss them."

"They are friends. They cannot return to Nottingham. We must be content with visits."

"Lord Cerne will not allow a visit from his lady to here. Too dangerous. You can visit her at the camp in Sherwood."

Ellen shook her head and didn't try an explanation. *Could a long-lived Faerie experience loss?*

Eventually, he said, "Your final feast will occur on the Full Moon."

Final? "Should I know anything of your guest?"

"Please her, and all will be well."

*If I don't please her? Is that the reason he says **final**?* "Who is she?"

"She who rules Underhill. I serve her. She has heard of the Yule feasts that the earl Cherdley will have. He invites many barons and knights. She wishes to experience such a feast."

"The dinner I serve will be a poor approximation of the earl's feast. No song and dance, no jesters and minstrels."

"She wishes to taste the best of human food. You will provide her with this wish."

"Did you convince her to eat mortal food? Lord Fenric—."

"I have told you that I am no lord. Merely a sentinel. Come, Plain Ellen Best, you worry needlessly."

Ellen didn't think worry was needless.

"I will bring a portion of a forest boar three nights before the Full Moon. Will this be sufficient time? You will use the silver coins for needed supplies."

"Time enough," she muttered, her mind twisting over different dishes for this duchess.

He tilted his head, as if he heard beyond her ken. "I must leave. My bow is needed."

He did not tarry on his going.

Plans for the feast for the Faerie duchess preoccupied Ellen.

A cake, she decided. One with whiskey to keep it fresh. She needed dried fruits and nuts and a trip to the Golden Arrow for the inn's best whiskey before she was ready for the baking.

An earl's feast would be a celebration of dressed boars and game birds as well as an artfully staged swan, so majestic in life, so pathetic in death. A young cockerel, tender of flesh, was a better choice. The individual pieces of the meaty flesh she would wrap in an eggy dough. The other pieces could go into a cheesy dish with diced parsnips.

She filled the passing days gathering supplies. She planned a clear broth, delicately flavored, for the first course; a bitter sallet after the cockerel, sweetened carrots to serve with the roasted boar. Shops for her first purchases, then the market. The silver coins diminished.

Darkness came early this close to the Winter Solstice and the shortest day, hastened by lowered clouds and swirling snowflakes. Ellen walked home from market, puzzling over her order of cooking for the next day.

Rustling in the bushes disrupted her. She paused and peered at the brambles, tangled canes that held no berries and only straggling leaves. The rustling came again, a little further on.

Then a hare jumped out and bounded along the path verging the forest.

Ellen laughed, her nerves as jumpy as the hare.

Once the roast miraculously appeared, surprising her with its glow, she worked diligently to prepare the dishes she'd planned. The fresh aroma of bay and cedar betrayed that Fenric had lingered after his delivery. She wondered the reason while she prepped the pork.

She intended to slow-cook the bulk of the roast and craft a minced pie with apples and onions. Leaves and acorns would decorate the pastry.

Ellen set to work with a will, for the boar roast would need all three days, even after removing the meat for the mince. Four meat dishes, servings of vegetables, pastry tasteful and artful, a cake—surely that was enough for a Yule feast.

Once the aroma of roasting boar started, it filled the hut, overwhelming all other odors. If Fenric had stood before her, she wouldn't have caught his fresh scent over the thick, mouth-watering smell of cooking pork.

.~.~.~.

Cold Moon rose bright and full, a silvery orb that displayed its dragon head.

The table with its goblets, the clay flagon of unending wine, pewter plates and utensils looked a poor setting for a duchess, especially a Faerie duchess.

Ellen ventured into Melly's dormant garden. The red-berried holly at the corner offered up several branches to her knife. When she came in with her finds, a white-haired man sat at table, his back to her. Had Fenric arrived?

But no, the Faerie's hair was a silvery cascade, not a grizzled wiry tangle.

A hand struck the middle of her back, shoving her into the

room.

She staggered forward, fetching up against the table, pricking her fingers on the sharp spines of the holly leaves.

The man turned. His pocked and weathered face had a mashed nose and a blackened eye. She recognized him. A robber of Nottingham, in the stocks for mischief during the last market.

Ellen reared backward, but the man behind her grabbed her nape and squeezed until she cried out. The old robber smiled. "No, Best Cook, we want all your coins. We'll take the food as well."

The pouches of her remaining silver and copper coins were on a shelf in the hidden root cellar. "I have no coins," she protested.

"You bought all this." He waved his hand at the roasting boar, the pots warming on the hearth, the minced pie on her workboard. "You been buying over a week. Fancy spices. Extra flour from the miller."

A lean greasy-haired man came into view. He picked up the bread she'd just removed from the oven rocked into the hearth. He broke off a hunk and crammed it into his mouth then tossed the loaf to the old robber. "S'good."

"You got coins left. You gotta have coins."

"I have nothing. I spent it all."

A blade flashed beside her face, and Ellen's eyes bulged.

"Let me play a bit," the man behind her said. "She'll tell us anything you want."

"No," she moaned.

"No," the old robber agreed. "We just want her coins and the food."

"She'll tell on us." He twisted his grip on her nape, wringing another cry from her. "The guards'll come after us."

The old man tapped her cheek. "She won't talk to them. Will you, Best Cook? Not after what we'll do afore we leave."

She whipped up the holly and slashed it across his face.

The man behind jerked her back then slung her sideways. She crashed into her workboard, past the man still chewing. Dropping the holly, Ellen grabbed the bowl for grinding spices and flung it. He ducked then vanished. Ignoring the commotion behind her, she grabbed her butcher knife and whirled to start a defense.

Fenric blocked her view. Back to her, his silvery hair unmussed, he held a glowing sword in guard position.

Beyond him stood a Faer lady, all silver and ice, steely armor and moon-touched leathers, her blade also glowing with power.

And the three robbers lay on the floor, stilly humps.

The table setting looked untouched, neither flagon nor goblets overturned, plates and utensils not shifted from position.

Fenric flicked his sword then sheathed it. He turned to her … and gently took away her knife. It vanished from his hand. He cupped her cheek. "Are you injured?"

She inhaled sharply. She had been wrong. Even with the smell of cooked boar and the rancid sweat and coppery blood of the men, she still caught his bay and cedar scent. "I'm unhurt."

A sparkling, a cool tingle, started beneath his hand and spread throughout her. Fear receded. Warmth poured in with the Fae energy, all the way to her fingers and toes. The pricks from the holly stopped hurting. Her abused nape stopped pulsing pain.

"A good practice," the Faer lady said. She examined her sword blade, and with horror, Ellen saw the blood on it. The Faerie ran her finger over the blood then licked it. "You provide an intriguing *amuse bouche* to start this feast." Then those dark eyes shifted away from Ellen, to Fenric, and Ellen started breathing again. "You will deal with these, Sentinel."

"At once, your grace." He hoisted a dead robber and carried him out.

Ellen's wits rushed back. She curtsied deeply. "Your presence quite awes me, your grace. Please, do sit." She pulled out the best chair then poured wine, her hand shaking only a little. "Your sentinel provided this wine."

Before the Faerie took the chair, her steely armor melted into a snow-blue gown with a deep beribboned bodice and full skirts covered with snowflakes and ice crystals.

Ellen rushed to serve the clear broth. When she brought the bowls to the table, Fenric sat opposite his duchess. The robbers were gone, only a memory now.

After the courses came the whiskeyed cake with a stout creamed tea, and the duchess demanded a second serving and then a third. With Fenric's appetite joined to the lady, little remained for Ellen's own dinner.

Eventually, the duchess rose from the table. She complimented Ellen on the pleasure of her dishes for the feast, "both intentional and unintentional." Her eyes glittered, and a wicked smile quirked her pale lips. "You are welcome to meet the cooks in Underhill at any time, Ellen Best. I would enjoy tasting what you will create with finer ingredients."

Ellen sank low. "I am honored, your grace."

A blinding light appeared around the duchess. When it faded, she was gone.

Fenric remained. "Her grace is well pleased."

Thank God didn't seem the right words to say to a pagan Faerie. She stumbled into "She did seem to enjoy every dish, especially the cake."

"She especially enjoyed the first sweet taste," Fenric laughed.

Ellen recalled the duchess licking blood from her finger.

"Where are they?" she asked hoarsely.

"They are ash. You need not worry. You have fulfilled your bargain, Plain Ellen Best. I must leave now. You may expect me at the next new moon." He was gone before she replied, not vanishing as the duchess had but leaving through the door. Cold night air and snowflakes rushed in, and she hurried to shut and bar the door.

With the two Faerie gone, the room seemed darker.

Yet touches of light remained, glowing softly, the goblets on the table, on her workboard, on the shelves that held her spices, on the boxes below that held flour and sugar.

A pouch of coins rested on the table. Gold coins spilled from it.

When she investigated, the plain pewter goblets and plates and bowls were now silver, the spoons and knives looked like steel. When she lifted down her spice jars, they were filled, as were her flour box and the formerly empty sugar box.

Those light-glowing supplies never ran out, no matter how much she used from them.

The three pouches of coins remained hidden in the root cellar. She rarely touched them. They also never emptied.

.~.~.~.~.~.

Note for the Reader

The pumpkin gourd that Ellen cooked into pies is not the pumpkin that we know today. That is an American plant, unknown anywhere in Europe in the Middle Ages.

The pumpkin gourd is an official term that references a *Cucurbita pepo* or the calabash gourd or (simply) gourd. The young form of these gourds is considered edible.

When we found no references to taste, we decided to treat the pumpkin gourd as we would the modern pumpkin.

Friar Tuck and the Faerie at the Pool

Brother Jerome broke off another hunk of bread. "Good," he said and waved the remainder of the loaf.

"Eat it soon," Friar Tuck urged. "In this heat it will grow stale and lose flavor."

The bone-thin hermit sniffed the air then said with a decisiveness at odds with his usual hesitant air, "Won't be hot tomorrow. Frost." Then he touched the pouch on the bench. "Mushrooms. More next time."

"Many brothers will appreciate your contribution, Brother Jerome."

"Which one made the bread? My thanks to him."

"That's not from the Abbey. Cook by the name of Ellen Best. Her meat pasties are very fine." He hastened to add, "I know you've sworn off meat, so I did not bring one to you."

The hermit's beginning frown faded. "May the good Lord bless this woman for her donation to the Abbey, and an additional blessing on you, my brother, for remembering my calling to this forest anchorage."

After stacking boxes and jugs in the hermitage, Tuck took his leave of the old man. He left the supplies for Robin Hood's camp hidden under a tarp. The old man, busy shifting supplies to his own organization, never spotted them.

He tugged his mule to the forest trail, a narrow path off the King's Road through Sherwood Forest. Few of his Abbey fellows wanted to venture into the forest, known for its outlaws and thieves. Tuck didn't worry about them. He had friends among the former, and thieves didn't target humble holy friars who had sworn poverty.

Within two miles, the day's heat began to burn through his system. Sweat trickled from his scalp, down his back and pits, from his soles. His sandals caught the grit from the road and trapped it, grinding at the calluses on his feet.

And Tuck remembered the pool that Jack Greenleaf had mentioned on his last visit to Robin's camp, deep in Sherwood Forest.

His mule suffered in the heat, and he promised cool spring water. The animal picked up its plodding pace. At the marker Jack had described, the trunks of three trees grown together, they left the main road and descended along a winding path. Jack had described the pool as surrounded by stacked boulders. Giant oaks and beeches towered over the little cleft. When the ground steepened its descent, Tuck chocked the wheels and unhitched the mule then followed the path.

At first he saw only the boulders. The coolness of the air was all that kept him tugging the mule forward. Then the path reached bottom and ventured around a stack of three boulders, and the pool opened before him. He heard muffled singing, a woman, but he saw no one.

The boulders encircled the pool on three sides. A sloping shelf of rock offered a tiny shore for the pool. The water looked clear and cold and deep. A spring, here in the forest, but he spied no outlet for the water. The calm water reflected the surrounding rocks, the leaves overhead, the patches of blue sky winking through the tree canopy.

He let the mule drink while he looked around. He no longer heard anyone singing, just birds, the wrens with their loud trills, the sad single note of the robin, blackcaps and thrushes melding their songs. Unable to resist longer, Tuck dropped to his knees. Beside the mule's dipping nose, he doused his head.

And heard the muffled singing again.

He tossed his head back, slinging water as his curly hair plastered to his scalp. The singing had stopped again. He cupped his hand and bent lower to drink. His woolen robe stuck to his sweaty skin.

When the mule had drunk his fill, Tuck tugged him away from the spring. He didn't want the animal to leave droppings near the clear water. He found a place to tie the mule, well off the path—although the mule's braying would attract anyone.

Tuck shed his sandals. The water at the sloping shelf barely covered his feet. He waded to the edge of the shelf and sat on a lower rock and dipped his feet and lower limbs into the water. There, now he felt the spring's chill. Feet dangling, he tried to remember everything he wanted to tell Robin and Little John about the new sheriff of Nottingham. The day's heat seemed to have burnt out his plans. The cold of the water promised a restoration.

But sweat still trickled down his back.

Tuck stood and shucked his heavy wool friar's robe. Then he dove into the spring. The cold water was silky smooth. The water's freedom recalled his boyhood, before his parents had died, before the monastery welcomed orphans inside its hallowed walls.

He floated, staring up at the leaves and the glimpses of blue. Arms outstretched, feet moving only enough to maintain buoyancy, he drifted, body and mind and soul at peace.

Then hands fastened on his slight shoulders and shoved him under.

He sucked in water. Frantically, he grabbed the water and paddled hard, propelling himself up. He came up sputtering.

Hands pushed him under again.

A woman laughed, a tinkling trill.

Tuck flailed. One hand struck another body in the cold water. He opened his eyes. Long hair, the color of moonshine, swirled before him. He saw the flash of pale flesh. The woman.

He beat his feet, reached with his hands, and gained the surface. Dragging in great gulps of air, he looked for the woman, waiting for her to surface.

She never did.

He swirled around—but she was nowhere in the pool. The water surged and splashed from his movements.

He hadn't imagined those hands shoving him under.

Tuck swam to the edge, found a toehold. The sloping shelf was on the other side of the pool. He grabbed rock then submerged to peer under the water.

The water tingled in his open eyes. Sunlight penetrated deep into the pool. The clear water offered no obstruction. Encircling layers of rock offered shelves and ledges, hiding places for fish—but fish didn't live in this spring. No matter how long he looked—he surfaced twice before sinking back, still clinging to sturdy rock—he couldn't see the bottom.

Nor did he see the woman.

He propped an arm on the slanting rock where he'd come up and just drifted, trying to cast aside the puzzle of the woman. His delivery of supplies would take only a few hours. He would stay the night at Robin's camp and return to the Abbey tomorrow. He had time to investigate.

Trilling laughter came again. Behind him.

Before he could turn, hands grabbed his ankles and jerked.

He slipped off his perch and sank deep. The shackling hands towed him deeper.

Tuck opened his eyes and looked down.

The woman was there, her hair whorling around her in the current-less water, her body pale against the blue depths of the spring. She towed him rapidly.

He kicked. She lost her grip—or maybe she released him. The woman shot past him on her way to the surface.

He pushed off a ledge, for she hadn't towed him away from the edge. Propelled to the surface, he looked for her—but she had disappeared again.

He slicked back his hair. "Lady," he called. "I mean no harm."

No answer. The water was empty save for him. No one perched on the boulders stacked around the spring.

He swam for the sloping shelf. The rock extended into the water, beyond the rocks under it. The cold of the spring had leached all warmth from his body. He braced his hands on the shelf to lever up.

"How do you mean 'no harm'?" she called. "You are here, in my pool."

Tuck slipped and surged back into the water. His head stayed up. He shivered. "I mean no harm to you or this place, Lady. The day was hot. The pool was inviting. I thank you for its use. I will leave now."

A flash from a high boulder. Then it landed on a lower boulder. Then the flash reached the shelf and blinded him. He blinked rapidly.

The woman stood before him.

Silver hair, miraculously dry, hid her body but not her pale legs. Her limbs were long and thin, fragile. She wasn't weak; she'd had strength enough to send him under. Her bones were willowy. Human limbs were sturdy.

But she wasn't human. She was Faerie.

The chill that shivered through him had nothing to do with the cold water.

Dark eyes peered at him. Tuck's angle below her increased the slanting angle of her features, yet her strange beauty fascinated him.

Too late he remembered his vows of chastity and looked away. Her image had burned into his mind, into his heart, into his manhood, stirring even in the icy water. *That* had to be magic.

Panicking, he lunged backward. The water accepted him, supported him, and he turned and sliced through it.

A splash. The woman surfaced beside him. He stopped swimming, stopped trying to reach the other side, and tread water. No one escaped a Faerie.

She was wondrous strange, not human yet quite lovely. "Why are you in my pool?"

Her musical voice had harmonies that charmed. Tuck gripped the wooden cross on its leather thong around his neck and wished it were made of iron nails. Iron burned Faeries. He was fully erect, desire pounding through him. Her magic, forcing his desire. He could want her, aye; but he feared her more.

He refused to reach for her. "The day is hot. The water is cool. I intended no offense, Lady."

She elevated in the water, more magic that lifted her torso above the water. The Faerie tossed her long hair, revealing her pert breasts, her shapely waist curving to hips, hinting at the prize below. She was perfect. Magic didn't force all his desire.

Tuck dragged his gaze back to those depthless black eyes that watched him narrowly.

"You do not want me?"

"I am a monk," he choked.

She sank in the water. Her hands touched his chest, petting the wiry pelt there then shifting to clasp his shoulders. She drifted close, her body brushing against his. The magic desire released him. Her grip tightened—then she thrust him under the water again.

He heard her trilling laughter as she pushed him lower and lower. Tendrils of hair wrapped around him, blinding him. Her legs tangled with his.

Her mouth touched his, opened over his, forced her air into his lungs. The world darkened. He saw only her, her pale skin shining in the shadowed water, her eyes dark in her beautiful face.

Then she released him. She swam away.

Once he surfaced, she gripped one of his hands and tugged him to the side. She levitated him from the water, up to the highest of the encircling boulders.

Contact with air had dried her hair and body, but water

sluiced from Tuck. Even in the hot air of this last-of-summer day, he shivered. He lay on his back and dragged in breaths. The green leaves still hid the sky. A wind had lifted. It blew the branches of the tall beeches, admitting flickers of sunshine.

All energy had sapped from Tuck. He felt like a wrung-out rag, used and discarded. The rock was hard under him, but he couldn't displace a floating feeling. *Am I still in the water? Am I dead?* His fingers scrabbled on the rough rock, seeking a grip, seeking anything substantial that he could cling to.

Then wind drifted over his chilled skin. The shivers increased. Why hadn't the Faerie killed him after she finished her cruel game? What more would he have to endure from her?

He squeezed his eyes shut. Why was it so hard to pray, to remember a prayer? He searched for the *Gloria Patri,* for *Te Deum*, for the Our Father. Fragments of the prayers floated in his mind, but the words refused to reach his tongue.

Then she loomed over him. She dropped his wool robe and sandals on the other side of the boulder. To recover them, he would have to reach around her. Tuck didn't want to fight her.

He didn't know why she wanted him naked. Why did she want him here at all? Did she want to shame him? Humiliate him? Punish him for trespass at her forest pool?

He knew only one answer. Faeries played with their victims.

He didn't like being a mouse.

Tuck sat up. He drew up his knees and wrapped his arms around them.

His shielding attempt was futile, for she said, "You still desire me?"

"Lady, you are lovely, wondrous strange and beautiful."

Her smile didn't ease his fright.

"You want me, but you do not touch me."

"No, my lady. That is against my vows."

"Vows. You say you are a monk. I know this word. You are a

holy man. What is your name? Tell me quick."

"Tuck. Friar Tuck."

"Friar. What is this word?"

"A special kind of monk. I have missions outside the Abbey."

"Into our bright forest."

He tucked in his scruffy chin. "I visit Robin Hood's camp and Brother Jerome in his hermitage."

"Robin Hood I hear of. Greenleaf and Scarlet. They have Faeries for friends. I did not think that possible. I learn many things are possible—including a man who does not snatch up what he desires."

She cast a small smile at Tuck. It lacked the bared teeth of her earlier smiles. He liked it. It was friendlier, somehow, not predatory.

"I do not know this word *hermitage*. What is this?"

"Brother Jerome is a hermit, a monk who consecrates himself to God by living alone. The tiny cell in which he lives is called a hermitage. In the past, monks were bricked into their cells. The abbot refused that for Jerome."

"Abbot?" She dropped to the rock beside him, so close his chilled flesh felt the warmth from her skin.

"The leader of our abbey is an abbot."

She shifted to sit cross-legged before him. "I know an abbot," and she laughed. "I think he wishes that he does not know me."

"Abbot? Abbot Linus?"

"That is the name he gave me."

Abbot Linus had disappeared last spring. He'd left on an *eyre* to the churches that reported to Thurgarten Abbey. When he didn't return at the appointed time, the Prior had waited another fortnight then sent three monks to search. Tuck had volunteered to search in Sherwood; the prior had ignored him. No words of the abbot had yet been received.

"Where is Abbot Linus?"

She trilled a laugh. "You do not know?"

"Is he dead?"

"He lives, so far. He is amusing."

Tuck shivered at her second laugh, cruel, malicious mischief, not gleeful humor. Here was the danger of Faeries. "Lady, is he nearby?"

"Near if you know the way, never to be found if you do not."

"Can I reach him if I swim to the bottom of your spring?"

Her laughter faded. "That is a way. It is not the best way. You would be injured if you took that way without me. Perchance you would die. I am not ready for you to die, Friar Tuck. Do not seek him that way."

And Tuck knew that Abbot Linus was in the Faer land. Underhill, he'd heard a few in Robin's camp call it. "Lady, the abbot is needed at the Abbey."

"For truth he is needed? I thought him merely a man who shouted orders and demanded others to wait upon him."

That sounded very much like Linus and one reason that Tuck had volunteered to be a friar. He didn't know, but he reckoned Brother Jerome had requested his hermitage for the same reason.

"Perchance I will release him." She gave a sly look from the corners of her eyes. "When he has worked out his penance."

"Penance?"

"That is the word, aye? When a human commits a sin and atones through many trials. This abbot taught me that word."

A sin? What crime had the abbot committed? Tuck mentally ran through the Commandments and the vows of service to the church. His order had the additional vows of poverty, charity, and chastity. Long ago he had cynically acknowledged that the abbey's leadership did not follow the first vow. The prior and his heavy hand of discipline broke the second vow, and the monks who reported to Abbot Linus and Prior Clement imitated their leaders.

From the Faerie's sly smile and her state of undress, he guessed the abbot had tried to break the third vow. "The abbot came to this pool. Did he assault you? Did he hurt you?" Beauty and eldritch strange as she was, the Faerie's thin bones would not withstand a mortal man's muscles. He'd experienced her strength underwater, but water had a way of canceling a man's advantage when a woman seized the upper hand. She had thrust him underwater, grabbed his ankles and towed him deeper. "Did he hurt you?" Tuck persisted.

"I am not a mortal woman. He can not harm me. My greater strength shocked him. He tried to fight me. Me! A Faerie! Then he shouted at me, words I do not know. He had a little wooden thing that he struck a rock with. It broke." Her mischievous grin flashed. She held out a hand and opened it. "The pieces are here. Do you want them, Friar Tuck?"

Tuck stared at the ruined wooden cross.

Abbot Linus had tried to damn the Faerie. That wouldn't work with pagans. Did Faeries even acknowledge God in his triune form? He refused to take the cross pieces. Of a surety, the abbot had broken all three vows of the order. He shuddered, wondering what punishments the Faeries required. "That was . . . . I regret that he no longer has it to give him comfort."

She flicked her hand. The pieces disappeared in a sparkling flash. "The duchess allowed him to keep his bejeweled pendant. He blubbers over it when he is not . . . otherwise employed."

Tuck didn't know how to respond. The Faerie looked expectant. Did she *want* him to ask how Linus was *otherwise employed*? He dared not. He wanted no mental image of the punishment inflicted by Faeries. "Did you drown him?"

"He did not enter the pool, not then. He fell upon me and tried to rut me like an animal. He needed punishment, a lesson to learn. He is not the ruler of this forest. Nor are the other men who come to this pool, swaggering braggarts. You are not like this abbot. When I saw you garbed as he, Tuck, I expected you to be like him." She tilted her head, a fall of silver hair burnishing as it caught the sun's radiance. "You are not like the other men either, men who think they own our bright forest. Nor are you like the others, the ones who show proper respect. They please our duchess. Lord Cerne does not need to hunt them. Do you know these other men? They call themselves outlaws, but I think they are not outside the law. This is what *outlaw* means, aye?"

"You're talking of Robin Hood and his men?"

"Robin. Aye, they name him leader. And a giant of a man that they call Little. One they call Scarlet for his fox-red hair. Greenleaf."

Tuck knew each man she named. The first others that she had mentioned, were they the rangers, the foresters? Were they also in Underhill, experiencing punishment for their crimes?

"Should you visit Underhill, Friar Tuck, I do not think you will curl into a ball and blubber and offer bargains that you have no hope of repaying."

"Never bargain with a Faerie," he responded immediately.

She laughed. "A good rule for humans, aye?" Humor filled this laugh, as it had not all her others. "I do not think many humans are wise."

"No, we are not," he answered dryly.

Her chin lifted. Her gaze cut to the path that led to the pool. She stood. Clothes magically covered her, a peasant woman's heavy skirt and blouse, a shawl wrapped crosswise over her breasts. Her appearance changed, beauty fading. She became pox-marked, her lips thinned to nothing, her nose mashed against her cheeks. Thick cloth covered her litheness. Her thin brown hair straggled. "Stay here, Friar Tuck. I wear this guise as a test for those who come. Some are kind. Many are not. See what happens. I think you judge me—."

"Lady, I would not dare."

She smiled. Her thin fingers grazed his head. "See and decide." Then she vanished.

Her words echoed. *A test. Some are kind. Many are not.*

Tuck had no doubt that Robin and his men fit the former category. And those who were not—. His abbot, ignoring all the lessons of Christ and the vow of charity for those less fortunate, the vow of chastity—for if that was the Faerie's guise when she encountered Linus, he had not been tempted by beauty. A love of power and control, cruelty and vice, those were his sins long before he encountered the Faerie at the pool.

The realization shamed him.

Tuck snatched up his brown robe and dropped it over his head. He slid his feet into his sandals. He gave a second's worry to his mule and the cart, then he heard voices.

Two men talking.

Tuck crouched on the boulder.

Rangers.

They held crossbows and carried their caps as they came down the trail.

They spotted the pool, for they stopped, exchanged a look, then raced to the water.

Like Tuck, the day's unexpected heat tempted them. They cast off their boots and weapons before they eased into the spring. Not swimmers, unlike Tuck, they didn't venture into the deeps but clung to the stony shelf. They splashed each other, laughing like boys.

He saw the Faerie in her guise before they did.

She came from the path, limping as if footsore, singing an old ballad. The men fell silent. They hauled themselves from the water.

He didn't hear the first exchange between the Faerie and them. She produced three apples, red ripe, and tossed one to each before taking a belt knife and cutting a slice from the one she'd kept.

The men ate their apples while they stood, water trickling out of their clothes.

Then they tossed the cores into the spring.

One said something that made the other laugh.

The Faerie's eyes opened wide. She tossed her scarcely eaten apple into bushes and held the knife defensively before her.

Fear ran through Tuck.

They sprang for the woman. The knife was twisted from her hand and sent spinning into the water. They swung her around and pushed her over. She screamed.

Tuck leapt to his feet. He shouted.

The men didn't react.

He scrambled off the boulder. His sandals slipped halfway down, and he plunged into the icy water. He flailed for the surface. The wool stretched, wrapping his arms, tangling his legs. He had to fight to swim upwards.

The sun blazed, blinding him. He couldn't see the Faerie or the men. His great splash into the pool had surely surprised them, stopped their assault on her. He swiped water from his face and looked around, but they still weren't in view. A fog veiled the spring, obscuring the path and the highest of the boulders.

He struck for the stony shelf.

When he pulled himself from the water, the brown wool flapping around him, he heard them, saw them. They had the Faerie on the ground. One tossed up her skirt. The other twisted her hair. She had fallen silent.

"Stop!" he shouted. "Stop! Have mercy!"

Neither man turned.

His youth spent in the monastery, he had little experience with fighting. The monks had squelched that in the orphans taken inside their walls. Tuck didn't launch himself at the men. He fell into them. The result was the same. He disrupted their assault, and they turned on him.

A fist swung. He ducked. He didn't duck the second punch. His face exploded with pain as he reeled back and fell into the bushes. Brambles pricked through the wool and snagged it, restraining him. Half-blinded, he tried to see what was happening with the Faerie, but the punch had misted grey over his sight.

He heard a splash before he extracted himself.

Then he heard whimpering.

And the grey mist cleared.

Tuck tore away from the last of the brambles.

The Faerie, no longer disguised, bent over one man on his knees. She had a dagger at his neck, blood beading where the point pricked his skin. Tuck had misjudged her strength, matching Faer to mortal woman.

Splashing came behind him. The other man flailed in the water, trying to reach the shelf.

When Tuck started for the pool, the Faerie snapped, "Do not, Tuck."

He stopped. Hands hanging, the brown robe stretched uncomfortably long and wide, he turned to the Faerie. "I saw."

"Did you decide?"

What could he say? He had vows. Years of lessons. Turn the cheek was not the least of them. The Faerie had tricked them, but she hadn't drawn them into her trap. They chose to commit a sin. They took those steps. Only her Faer strength and wiliness prevented a second, greater sin.

The splashing ended. Water flooded into the pool. That man cursed then stopped as he saw the difference in the Faerie, beauty restored, wondrous strange. "Odo, get up," he snapped.

Odo whimpered.

He growled like a feral dog. "Get outta m'way, monk."

Face pulsing with pain, Tuck shook his head. "Go you away from here. Never come back."

The man raised his fists.

Tuck plowed forward, head down like a determined ox. A fist knocked his head, the other punched his shoulder, then he rammed into the man. Behind Tuck was a whoosh, a gust that fluttered through his wet woolen robe. He gained more energy and surged forward, pushing the ranger back to the pool. The man fell in with a splash.

Tuck nearly tumbled in. One foot in the water, he stopped before he fell over.

The man splashed and cursed, cursed and splashed.

The water swirled, darkened, became an eddy that sucked the man into its center. He screamed before he disappeared into the vortex.

The water swirled a breath longer, then it slowed, stilled. Once more it reflected the boulders, the trees, the glimpses of sky.

Of the man there was no sign.

Tuck stared and stared, but he saw nothing. When he turned back, Odo had also gone.

To Underhill. To serve penance for their sins. Like Abbot Linus.

The Faerie remained.

She smiled, that malicious one that frightened him. "Well met, Friar Tuck. I must go. I have visitors to introduce."

He didn't ask questions. He bowed. "Lady."

"Will you come again to my pool?"

"Will I be able to find it?" he countered.

That trilling laugh rippled out. "If you seek, you will find. You alone, Tuck. Perchance I will return your abbot soon."

"That can wait a while."

She laughed, a full-bodied laugh that held real humor. "Perchance I will return him to a different location. He seeks a *Palatium Lateranense*. He thinks he will be safe there. Shall I take him to this place, Tuck?"

The idea of a Faerie invading the home of the Pope appalled him. When she saw his shock, she laughed again.

.~.~.~.

After she had gone, Tuck tossed the rangers' bows into the back of his cart and began his long-delayed journey to Robin's camp, deeper in Sherwood.

Our forest, she had called it.

He arrived as twilight fell. After dispensing his supplies and visiting those who were sick or needed a quiet word, he joined those gathered around the campfire. He settled beside Jack Greenleaf.

Jack handed him the goatskin. Tuck drank deep of the ale. As he wiped his mouth on the sleeve of his dry-shrunken robe, Jack said, "Saw you heading to the hermit's this morning. Expected you earlier. He doing well?"

"Very well. The hermitage suits him." He passed the ale on before he added, "Remember that pool you told me about?"

Already a still man, Jack stilled even more. "I remember, aye. Did you go there? What did you think of it?"

Tuck clasped his knees. "I have met beauty and been mortally terrified."

Alan-a-Dale & the Harp of Elandrielle

Pain consumed him. It had no center. It ratcheted through him.

He remembered.

He didn't want to. He wished to cast memory into oblivion. The solid punches to his face and gut, the sharp clips to his ears, the kicks when he rolled on the stone-cold ground.

The cracks as they broke bones.

The humiliation when he begged them to stop.

The pain was easier to bear than *that* memory.

But Alan was conscious now. The pain gave no ease—nor did his senses.

A steady rumbling jarred him. Wooden cart wheels. Cold, cold all through him, so cold he felt locked in ice. Whispered voices.

Then one clear voice saying "Here. Drop him here. We gotta get back."

He knew that voice, the one he didn't want to hear. Bartlesby. His chief rival in the song competition. Good but not good enough against Alan. Another night of music would prove that.

If he still lived for the second and final night of the competition.

A clamber into the cart set it rocking, and Alan groaned.

"He's awake," Oswent shouted. Another competitor. Had the top four joined against him?

"Shut yer trap," another said. Alan recognized that voice as well. Old Thom, the host at the Tinker's Wife. Alan owed him money. *Did Thom take the coins out of my hide?* "Roll `im out."

Rough hands seized him, jerked him around, then dumped him out of the cart.

The shock of pain cast him into blackness.

.~.~.~.

Alan woke again to pain, to bright sunlight penetrating through his eyelids, to the juddering rumble of a cart.

A cheerful whistle. Trills and chirps from the birds that hadn't flown away for winter.

The cold frosty air of morning.

He turned his head. Everything reeled and veered.

The cart lifted over then dropped hard.

Alan moaned then sank into blessed unconsciousness.

.~.~.~.

Pain remained a constant companion. Consciousness was not. When he woke again, Alan wished for the blankness of elsewhere. He lay in aching misery. His whole body pulsed with it, some aches piercing, some throbbing, some shooting fire through him, some wrenching. He writhed through those, which set up a host of the others.

"You see?" a man asked.

Alan seized on the unknown voice, something to concentrate on rather than his unwanted companion.

"You alone, Tuck. You alone."

A woman. The harmonies in her voice soothed. Alan longed to hear more.

"He needs help, Lady. He is far beyond my simple cures."

"I am no healer, Tuck. This will help . . . but not his greater hurts."

"I prayed you could help him. He did not deserve this. No one does."

She didn't answer, and an ache throbbed while Alan waited.

"I know someone," the lady admitted. "She may refuse."

"That is all I ask."

Alan heard a whoosh. A flash penetrated his swollen eyes.

Then the cart shifted. He sensed someone beside him. His head was lifted. Cold metal touched his lips.

"Here. Drink."

Wine. Good wine, better than he had ever tasted. He swallowed a mouthful, two, a third, then shut his lips. The cup was taken away.

"I bandaged what needed it," the man said. "Bound your fingers. The bruises will fade. The bones will heal. The swelling around your eyes already goes down. I fear you have internal troubles, though. Do not move unless you must."

Do not move. Alan wished he could laugh. He just moaned.

"What is your name?"

"Alan," he whispered on a breath. "Alan-a-Dale" took two more breaths.

"I am Friar Tuck."

"Who—?"

"A friend. We are at her spring in Sherwood Forest." Rough wool brushed his skin, a minor scratch. "You will be warmer by the fire. Your legs are unharmed. If you can stand, I will help you there."

Alan nodded, but pain told that he was a fool. Still, he lifted a hand for help.

"Both hands," Tuck urged. "You should be lifted evenly."

The man grasped Alan's wrists. He pulled him up with ease, guided Alan's right hand to the side of the cart. Alan felt the edges of roughly planed wood. When Tuck grabbed Alan's ankles to slide him over the cart's bottom, Alan reached for the other side. Only then did he realize his left hand was bound up.

"Best not use the left," the man advised. He inexorably drew Alan to the cart's back as he gasped with pangs and wrenches. "Stand."

He steadied Alan. Grabbing his right elbow, Tuck led him away from the cart.

One eye half-slitted couldn't see the ground. The other was totally closed. Yet he heard birdsong, the ripple of water, the rasp of dry leaves still clinging to trees. The ground was soft dirt, rocks that his feet rolled over. The air was chill and clean. He heard fire crackling over wood but smelled no smoke. "What's the damage?" He wasn't certain that he wanted to know.

"Big rock here. Step over. Good. Well, ribs are the worst of it, I think. You got kicked. Your face is a mess, but a woman who loves you won't care that your nose is mashed."

"I don't—." He breathed through a spasm. "I don't make my living with my face."

"Good thing, then. Little bit further."

He waited, but Tuck didn't continue. Alan didn't want to ask about his hand. "Where are we? You said Sherwood. I haven't heard of a spring in Sherwood."

"Not many know of it."

"How far … from Nottingham?"

"Easy distance. Here. Turn." He guided Alan. "Sit here. It's not too low."

The seat was a boulder. Alan eased down. He landed before his legs scarcely bent. It would be easy for him to stand … if he could see where to go. "That woman, who is she?"

"A friend," Tuck said. "I pushed our friendship bringing you here, so be courteous. She doesn't do well with strangers. Hear me, Alan?"

"I hear. Not much I *can* do like this." His right hand swept his body.

"You got a mouth. She's a lady. Treat her with courtesy."

Alan heard him poking at the fire. He waited, but the truth of the worst of his injuries would have to be heard. "Why is my hand wrapped up?"

"I heard you singing last night, at the earl's banquet." Tuck started with a round-about answer. "I came out with the kitchen staff to listen to the competition. You were better than the others. Should have won outright last night. You know who did this?"

That was an easy answer, even if Alan had only heard them after they jumped him in the dark lane that he'd taken for a shortcut. "My rivals and a man I owe money to."

"You would have won the prize. You could have paid him off then."

"That's what I promised to do." He paid for his huffed laugh with a spasm of pain. "He likely wanted to keep me indebted to him. I was working—." He stopped and breathed through the next wrench. "I was working off my debt, singing at his tavern. The Tinker's Wife."

"Old Thom? He doesn't have a lot of sense. Mess you up like this, and you can't entertain his customers."

"I can still sing."

"With those ribs, it will be hard to take deep breaths."

That was truth, but Alan had never credited Old Thom with any sense. "Where did you find me?"

"They dumped you in the forest. Just along the King's Road."

"How did … you find me?"

"Saw them coming back with an empty handcart. They were…. Let's say their laughter didn't sound like good fellowship."

He'd heard such laughter in the past. Never before, though, had it been directed his way.

A cup shoved into his right hand. "Hot. Take it slow. That weird taste is healing herbs."

Alan sipped. The warmth hit his stomach and gradually spread through his torso. "Herbs from your friend?"

"They work better than what's grown at the Abbey."

"Abbey? You're a monk. No. I remember. You said you were a friar."

"Nothing wrong with your memory."

Friar. Friar Tuck. Knowledge spread through him. He'd seen the brown-robed friar on errands in and about Nottingham. "Why bring me here? Why not the Abbey?"

"That's a set of other problems."

"Problems?" He drank more of the herb brew.

"The prior would have reported the beating to the Sheriff. The new Sheriff would have taken you into custody to get the whole story. Then he would have throw the men who beat you into the cell with you until the Assizes when a magistrate would sort the problem for him."

"That solves nothing. They would beat me daily."

"The complainant dead, the charges can be dropped. Unless you have the coin to pay a tithe to free yourself."

"The Sheriff wouldn't do that. He represents the law."

"It has happened." Tuck's curt words were more convincing than a full explanation with names and dates. "Drink up. The tea's getting cold. She should return soon."

Where had she gone? Alan sipped and recalled the whoosh as she'd left. What woman would live at a spring in the forest? She wasn't a healer. Where had she gone to find a healer?

The day had brightened. Though he could see little around him, he saw enough through slitted lids to know the sun had that blinding brightness of an early winter day. Its radiance warmed him. Circling trees might have lingering leaves, but enough had dropped to permit sunshine through the canopy.

He thought of the weeks needed to heal bones. He knew his ribs were cracked. How long before he could draw the deep breaths needed to sing the best ballads with their long-held notes? How long before he could fill his chest with the air needed to support the high-pitched notes?

Singing was only part of his talent.

His undamaged fingers tightened on the cooled tin cup. The men had broken his harp, the one he'd brought from Ireland in his grand idea to conquer England and take home a fat purse to demand the respect he deserved from his friends and family.

He had loved that harp. He slept with it tucked against his chest, lover-like. He kept it free of damp, wrapped in a special oilskin when he traveled from town to town.

Old Thom had likely claimed the oilskin along with Alan's hidden pouch of hard-earned coins and the rest of his belongings. Or Thom had divided the goods with Bartlesby and Oswent.

He tried to move his bound fingers. Pain shot out. He sensed no movement.

Alan blindly set down the cup. He didn't want the answer. He knew it already, but he needed it spoken. The earl of Cherdley's competition was lost to him; he accepted that. The purse of silver coins would never come to him. He could groan about that later. "Tuck, tell me the worst of it. How bad?"

"Bad."

"Tell me!"

"Broken fingers. Broken thumb. Broke the bones in your hand, too badly for me to set." The friar didn't say more. He didn't have to.

Broken fingers. One day Alan might recover some speed of his fingering of the harp strings. To recapture the speed he'd had, the speed that set him steps higher than his competitors—he'd never have that again. The bones in his hand—mended wrongly, they would fuse. He'd lose all ability to play.

He could teach his right hand to move as freely and as nimbly as his left, but that would take months.

How would he support himself for months? Singing at the Tinker's Wife?

How would he afford a replacement harp? Even a cheap one was beyond his current means.

Tears dripped from his swollen eyes.

Hopeless. All his dreams gone. Vanished in a few minutes of anger.

What would he give to walk into the earl's hall and take his place beside Bartlesby and Oswent and the other two who'd won spots in the final round of competition? What would he give to have the harp, to pluck beautiful melodies and contramelodies, to sing the haunting ballads and lively jigs of his home to these English?

Tuck pressed more tea upon him. Alan drank. The tea helped with the pain of his injuries.

Never the pain of his heart.

He was working through his third cup of Tuck's brew when he heard women talking.

"Stay here," Tuck said as he went to meet them. Alan wished he felt like asking *Where else am I to go?*

He sensed someone before him and lowered the cup before looking up.

"Were you fighting?" a woman asked. Her voice sounded odd, with harmonies that shouldn't have been possible.

"They jumped me. Dumped me in the forest when they were finished."

"How did you provoke them?"

"I placed above them in a song competition, the one the earl of Cherdley is holding this Yuletide." Warmth slid over his face. He blinked then realized that he could see, that his eyes were no longer swollen shut. He blinked again, and the woman swam into view. Pale skin and silver hair, yet she wasn't old. She had a freshness at odds with any age.

Faerie. He'd never before seen one. He'd not heard talk of them at any point during his time in England. At home, any talk of Faeries came with warnings. They enjoyed mischief. Many were malicious.

This Faer lady was eldritch eerie yet beautiful, dressed in flowing silk, flowers braided into her shimmering hair. Eyes so dark he couldn't see the centers.

She smiled.

Alan took a deep breath. Pain writhed through him.

She grasped his shoulder, and the pain ended. A coiling warmth invaded his chest. It spread throughout his torso. "Lady," he breathed.

"Tuck tells me that you sing and play the harp." She lightly touched his bandaged hand. "Not with this, I think."

"No. I may never play the harp again."

"No?"

"No. Broken bones never completely heal."

"Even with healing from a Faerie?"

Magical healing. Had she already healed his ribs? No, that pain was still there, muted. "Please, Lady, do not toy with me."

She laughed, a musical trill. "You have met my cousins, I think. I am not they. What will you give me, Alan-a-Dale, when I restore you?"

Faerie bargains are dangerous.

But to sing and play as he had—.

"Will you give me your firstborn?"

He stopped thinking of what he'd lost and started thinking of all the tales he'd heard of humans trapped in Faerland. "No!"

She laughed again. "Do not panic. I tease you. You know

this, aye?" Then her laughter died, her face becoming a solemn mask. "I must have something you value highly. I may not give unless I also receive."

"I have no coins. When I win the earl's competition—."

"Bah! Humans and their coins. That makes for a bad bargain."

"I have nothing to give and no hope of getting anything, without my ability to sing and play the harp."

"Perchance I should enrich my offering." Light flashed, and she held a harp similar to his. This one, though, had carved wood so light and polished that it shone like gold. The strings looked like silver wires, glistening in the sunlight. She ran light fingers over the strings. They sounded full and rich, resonant and harmonic. "This is similar to the harp that I offer for this competition."

Should this harp accompany his voice, Alan knew he would win every competition with the simplest of ballads. He wasn't certain his voice was worthy of the harp. "Lady—."

"Come. What have you to match my harp? I do not want your firstborn or your soul or even your life."

"The only thing of any value is my voice."

Those black eyes opened very wide. "You would give me your voice? Do you not need your voice?"

"It is the only thing of value that I have."

"Oh, you have a greater gift, but this I will accept. Perchance not in the way you expect." She struck her chest. "We have a bargain. You have Elandrielle's harp, and after this competition, I have your voice."

. ~ . ~ . ~ .

Alan slid into place beside the other balladeers. Two looked crestfallen at his appearance. Two looked sour, Bartlesby and

Oswent. Their ploy with Old Thom, to beat him up then haul his battered carcass into the forest, had failed.

Would they confront him? That would be an admission that they'd beaten him. Only remnant bruises remained as evidence. The Faerie had healed the broken bones, the deep pangs that spasmed through him, and the cracked ribs that seized his breaths.

He flexed the fingers of his left hand. No pain lingered. No stiffness attacked the joints. With the few notes he'd played as practice, he'd experienced no fumbling, no hesitation.

No pain lingered, at all.

The Faerie had left his face bruised, his nose mashed. The latter affected his top notes, but none of his planned songs had any of those.

He stroked the harp cradled in one arm. The sound of the strings hummed in his mind. The wood under his fingers was as silky smooth as tender flesh.

His eagerness for tonight's performance was partly the delight of songs done well, extending his own pleasure into the audience. A greater part of his eagerness, though, was a shamed glee at trouncing the rivals who had battered him.

The Faer lady had guessed at that vengeful relish.

Alan kept his mind firmly away from his bargain with the Faerie. Singing had been his companion from his childhood, when he first began to sing ballads with his mother. Once he knew the melody, she sang harmony, and the greater joy was singing together, their blended voices resonating in his head. He'd learned harp to recapture that joy, letting the harp sing the harmony.

After this competition, he would only have the harp. It would do.

The earl of Cherdley provided a dinner for contestants, but Alan was taut as a harp string and dared not eat.

The steward tolled off their order for the evening's

competition. Alan was first, not last as he preferred. As first, all others would be compared to him. Any of his mistakes would be magnified. His special flourishes on the harp might be forgotten.

If he lost, even though he'd bargained with a Faerie and used a magical instrument, he didn't know what he would do.

He wasn't even certain of the bargain's terms. Would he still lose his voice if he lost the competition?

Why would a Faerie want his voice?

With the first course of the Yule feast served, the steward escorted him to a bench, set center, with tables on three sides. He faced the earl and his young bride, the honored guests also on the raised dais. Knights and the Sheriff crowded the other tables with their ladies. Last night the listeners had heard numerous performers before Alan sang. They'd expected entertainment and quickly fallen silent to hear. He had to capture them immediately.

As the steward bowed then began his announcement of the competition, of the rules for the evening, and of the competitors, Alan revised the three songs that he'd intended to play.

His name announced, he bowed deeply then took the bench. Last evening each competitor spoke a few words. He did not do so tonight, and the others would be forced to follow the pattern he'd set. He'd give them no chance to win points with sympathy.

The bruises purpling his face and his clearly mashed nose would speak silently for sympathy. The others had no such obvious signs.

The chatter and laughter hurt his ears, yet he started into a lively jig. The rhythm caught their attention. Some clapped, some drummed on the table. Even the earl and his guests were toe-tapping the rhythm. Certain he had them, Alan launched into the song, a hero off to war and his sweet love waiting for his return.

His next song was a crowd-pleaser, with a chorus that listeners could sing: "Fol-de-rol-de-lay." *Good choice*, he knew, for servants took away and brought in the next course without the dinner guests breaking away from the song. He extended the song's length with a repetition of the first verse then the chorus sung three times.

The servants lingered in the archways to the kitchen and halls. He saw Tuck's golden curls. He stood with the servants, clapping the beat, joining in the chorus.

Alan had them and knew it.

When he played the first notes of his haunting ballad, the room hushed. He concentrated on the harp, on the glistening silver strings. A golden glow emanated from the instrument. He didn't know if that was magic or his imagination. He didn't care.

When his last clear note faded away, the hall stayed hushed.

Then the earl stood and applauded. The crowd joined in. Some shouted. Alan heard three whistles.

He bowed then walked from the hall with tears in his eyes.

As the evening progressed, he lingered in a side hall. He clutched the harp to his chest as he answered stray questions. He didn't listen to his competitors' performances. He wasn't certain he could concentrate enough to do so.

At the banquet's end, the steward lined up all five singers to receive the earl's verdict of winner. Alan stood straight, head lifted high, certain of the outcome but unwilling to smile arrogantly. The earl came around the table to present the prize. Alan accepted the purse then bowed low, but his drumming pu prevented him from hearing Lord Cherdley's congratulations. knew the other four slunk away from the line while he swept his cap and bowed to all three tables.

In the side hall his back was thumped, pints of celebrato were shared, and work singing at various inns were offered

His only thought was returning to the forest pool and p his side of the bargain to the Faer lady.

The frigid night woke him from his daze over his performance and celebration. The purse dragged heavily belt. The harp remained light, the golden wood reflectir moonlight. The strings glistened with moonshine.

Nottingham was quiet. Most of the residents woul

i

the castle, celebrating Yule and free food and drink far into the night.

When two men moved out of the shadows, Alan wasn't shocked. He stopped and cast a glance backward. A third shadow detached from the wall.

"Now then," one said, thumping a fist into his palm, "hand over that purse."

He didn't answer. He recognized Bartlesby. Defiance would gain him nothing. Obedience would confirm his weakness. Alan gripped the harp closer to his thudding heart.

"Come on then," said the man behind. Old Thom. "Do it now."

Alan turned his head. "What do you get out of this, Thom?"

"My share," the old man grumped.

"I won" was his only protest.

"And now we will," said Bartlesby.

Silent Oswent surprised him, darting forward to rip at the harp. The man slung it away, into the shadows.

"Careful," Thom cried. "There's good money in that. We can sell it on easy."

Bartlesby grabbed him, slung him into Oswent who shoved him to the ground. Alan rolled away as they kicked out.

A flash of light. Then Old Thom cried out. Alan didn't see the reason. He had curled up, giving his back to the kicks. This night the men wore softer shoes. They'd had wooden clogs last night.

Another lightning flash, yet he heard no thunder.

His hand snapped out and caught a foot. He grabbed the ankle with his left and twisted. A man crashed down. He yelped as light flashed again.

Then all fell silent.

Alan straightened. He saw the harp's soft glow and turned to

The Faer lady stood there. She smiled—a predator's toothy smile.

The three men had vanished. He didn't want to contemplate where they now were.

He looked away, hunting the harp, but it had vanished. His gaze came reluctantly back to the Faerie. Yanking off his cap, he swept a deep bow. "Lady. I am ready to pay my side of the bargain."

"Yet you no longer have my harp."

He peered into the shadows. "I don't know where it is."

The Faerie raised her arms, twirled—and he saw the ribcage shape in her body and harp strings in her flowing silver hair. The illusion shimmered away as she stopped twirling.

She laughed at his shock. "I enjoyed this evening, Alan-a-Dale. You have given me three new songs and three new playthings. A richness I did not expect. Payment enough for your side of our bargain. And I give you this." She waved a fragile-seeming hand. A harp appeared, and she came close to offer it.

With shock, he saw the nicks and notches accumulated over the past years. She had restored to him his old Irish harp. "Lady," he said shakily.

"My friend's friend Tuck will take you to people who can be trusted. Stay safe, Alan-a-Dale. No longer tempt shadows in the evening. Next full moon, you may see me again."

He chilled. "Lady?"

"My duchess enjoys fine singing. Together we would give a memorable evening." Then she swirled, gold shedding from her. The twirl narrowed, took on vines and flowers, then shot and shrank.

When he blinked, the moonsilver light had disappeared.

"Alan?"

He turned and saw the friar.

"Was there trouble?"

"Not now, Tuck, but I think I should be scarce in Nottingham for a while."

"Come with me. I will take you to friends."

"She said you would."

"As Elandrielle said, so we must do," Tuck said calmly. "You will like my friends, I promise."

Alan followed the friar through the dark streets. No one accosted them.

He hoped no one ever did again.

.~.~.~.~.~.

Thank You!

Thank you for reading our stories in the Wild Sherwood series. We hope you've enjoyed dipping into the Robin Hood legends and love the addition of the Faeries.

Edie says~

I've always enjoyed the legend of Robin Hood and his Merry Men. As yet, I haven't been disappointed in any of the versions that I've found—although I do have my favorites, including *Outlaws of Sherwood* by Robin McKinley, the British television series (for which I've never managed to see all the episodes), and the Walt Disney animated movie.

M. says~

For the past years I've concentrated on mysteries, but fantasy is also a great love. The Robin Hood characters have always interested me. Including Faeries, the dangerous ones of early British legend, those who ride the Wild Hunt, not the flower fairies and the sprites, those ideas intrigued me. Mixing Faeries with Robin Hood gave inspiration for more stories and novels.

Us again~

For various reasons, we began this series with short stories. The world is fun to explore, fun to write, and extra fun to finish.

Watch for more stories and novellas in Wild Sherwood.

. ~ . ~ . ~ .

Edie Roones and M.A. Lee are with Writers Ink Books. For any questions, comments, and speculations, please contact winkbooks@aol.com. Information and links are on the website

Writers Ink Books. Look for their titles at online distributors both nationally and internationally.

To receive information about M.'s writing and collaboration with Edie Roones, please subscribe to her seasonal newsletter. Contact either winkbooks@aol.com or use the following link to join the newsletter AND receive a free mystery short story featuring secondary characters from *Christmas with Death* >> https://dl.bookfunnel.com/wc84divkre

Edie has not yet plunged into the newsletter realm.

Please write a review.

Indie writers thrive on freely-given reviews. We're small beans here; we don't have the advertising budget of the Big Peeps. Of course, with *any* book that you enjoy, whether written by us or by anyone else, please share with other readers looking for escape from the dark stresses of life. That's the reason we write.

Titles by Edie Roones

Into Wild Sherwood ~ this anthology

Tod the Fox and the Faeries in the Ring

The Poisoner and the Faerie Huntsman

Friar Tuck and the Faerie at the Pool

Three Yule Feasts for the Faeries

Alan-a-Dale and the Harp of Elandrielle

The Seasons in Sansward Quarternary

Summer Sieges

Autumn Spells

Winter Sorcery

Spring Magicks (in the sketching stage)

Fiction by M.A. Lee

Into Death ~ Historical Mysteries featuring Isabella Newcombe (set 1919 and after) (full-length novels)

   Digging into Death

   Christmas with Death

   Portrait with Death

   "The Lion's Den" ~ a short story with side characters from *Christmas with Death*

Hearts in Hazard ~ Regency Mysteries and Suspense with a dash of Romance (full-length novels with slightly interwoven characters)

1 ~ *A Game of Secrets*

2 ~ *A Game of Spies*

3 ~ *A Game of Hearts*

4 ~ *The Danger of Secrets*

5 ~ *The Danger for Spies*

6 ~ *The Danger to Hearts*

7 ~ *The Key to Secrets*

8 ~ *The Key for Spies*

9 ~ *The Key with Hearts*

10 ~ *The Hazard of Secrets*

11 ~ *The Hazard for Spies*

12 ~ *The Hazard with Hearts*

Miss Beale Writes ~ a touch of gothic, a touch of mystery, a touch of paranormal

The Dark Lord

The Captive in Green (coming soon)

Visit Writers Ink Books

for more information about the writings

of Edie Roones and M.A. Lee.

Write to us at winkbooks@aol.com

www.ingramcontent.com/pod-product-compliance
Lightning Source LLC
Chambersburg PA
CBHW050832180626
46814CB00004B/1577